THE ADVENTURES OF THE
NEW CUT
GANG

www.randomhousechildrens.co.uk

PHILIP PULLMAN

THE ADVENTURES OF THE
NEW CUT GANG

THUNDERBOLT'S WAXWORK

THE GAS-FITTERS' BALL

ILLUSTRATED BY MARTIN BROWN

CORGI YEARLING

THE ADVENTURES OF THE NEW CUT GANG
A CORGI YEARLING BOOK 978 0 552 57214 9

First published in Great Britain by David Fickling Books,
when an imprint of Random House Children's Publishers UK
A Penguin Random House Company

Penguin
Random House
UK

David Fickling Books edition published 2011
This edition published 2015

3 5 7 9 10 8 6 4 2

Corgi Yearling Books are published by Random House Children's Publishers UK,
61–63 Uxbridge Road, London W5 5SA

www.**randomhousechildrens**.co.uk
www.**totallyrandombooks**.co.uk
www.**randomhouse**.co.uk

Addresses for companies within The Random House Group Limited can be found at:
www.randomhouse.co.uk/offices.htm

THE RANDOM HOUSE GROUP Limited Reg. No. 954009

A CIP catalogue record for this book is available from the British Library.

Penguin Random House is committed to a sustainable future for
our business, our readers and our planet. This book is made from
Forest Stewardship Council® certified paper.

Printed and bound in Great Britain by Clays Ltd, St Ives plc

Contents

Thunderbolt's Waxwork

Contents

One

Dippy's Ambition

Lambeth, 1894

The criminal career of Thunderbolt Dobney began on a foggy November evening outside the Waxwork Museum. Thunderbolt had never thought of himself as a criminal; he was a mild and scholarly youth. But he was a passionate collector of curiosities, and for some days now he had been filled with desire for the odd-shaped lump of lead belonging to Harry Fitchett, a boy in his class. Finally, after much bargaining, he had persuaded Harry to swap it for a length of catapult rubber.

The exchange took place under a hissing gaslight by the Waxworks entrance.

'This is stolen property, this lead,' said Harry. 'It come off that old statue of King Neptune outside the Lamb and Flag. *You* remember.'

The knowledge that he was holding a piece of criminal history added to Thunderbolt's pride. Harry ran off, twanging his length of rubber at the legs of passers-by, and Thunderbolt dropped the lead into his pocket with a guilty thrill.

The others, meanwhile, were gazing up at the poster advertising the latest attraction at the Waxworks.

'A victim of the Atrocious Death of a Thousand Cuts,' read Benny Kaminsky.

Benny was a stocky, dark-haired boy of eleven. When you saw Benny at first you took him for an ordinary boy. When you'd known him for half an hour you were convinced he was a genius. When you'd known him for a day you suspected he was the Devil, but by then it was too late: you were drawn in. Everyone who knew Benny was drawn in, because he was less like a boy than a whirlpool. The New Cut

Gang were proud to follow him.

Thunderbolt peered at the poster Benny was looking at.

'Ah! I read about that in the encyclopaedia,' he said. 'What they do is, they tie 'em up and slice bits off 'em with a razor. They start at the feet and work up. Takes *hours*,' he added enthusiastically, pushing his glasses up with a grimy finger.

'Well?' said Bridie. 'Are we going in or not?'

Bridie Malone was red-haired and red-tempered, and at least as fierce as Benny. Everywhere that Bridie went, her little brother Sharky Bob came too. He was a placid and benevolent child who would eat anything, and often did. The others didn't mind having Sharky about because they'd often won bets on his ability to chew up and swallow dog biscuits, champagne corks, fish heads and anything else the sporting citizens of Lambeth offered him.

He was plucking at Bridie's sleeve now.

'Dippy's selling chestnuts,' he said. 'I seen him just now. I likes chestnuts,' he added helpfully.

So did they all. The Death of a Thousand Cuts

forgotten, they streamed across the road and around the corner to Rummage's Emporium, where Dippy Hitchcock had set up his hot-chestnut stand. Rummage's Emporium took up several shop-fronts. It was the biggest store in Lambeth, and the windows were blazing with light and streaming with condensation. Old Dippy was selling some chestnuts to a customer who'd just come out, and he greeted the kids cheerfully.

'Three penn'orth, please, Dippy,' said Benny.

He had earned a shilling earlier that day by holding some horses for the Peretti Brothers (Removals, Funerals and Seaside Excursions). You got sixteen chestnuts for a penny, so that would mean twelve each. The kids stood around Dippy's little stove to eat them, fishing the smoking nuts out of the triangular twists of paper and rolling them between their palms to loosen the skin.

'You been to the Waxworks then?' said Dippy. 'I'd like to be a waxwork.'

'They don't make waxworks of hot-chestnut men,' said Thunderbolt. 'Only Kings and criminals and people like that.'

'I used to be a criminal,' said Dippy. 'I set out to be a pickpocket. But I had to give it up on account of me conscience.'

'Unless you're a celebrated murderer, it's not worth mentioning crime,' said Benny. 'Ain't you done anything else to make you famous, Dippy?'

Dippy rubbed his bristly jaw. 'No,' he said mournfully. 'But I'd love to be a waxwork. Make me feel me life had been worthwhile, somehow.'

Another customer came out of Rummage's and bought a pennyworth of chestnuts, paying with a sixpence. Bridie was interested in this waxwork talk, but even more interested in the nearest window, where a stout and shiny man called Mr Paget, the Gentleman's Outfitting Manager, was clambering about arranging a mannequin. Every time he lifted the arm into position and turned round to pick up some gloves from behind him, the arm fell down again, and he got more and more vexed and more and more shiny. The arm came up – the arm fell down; he dropped the gloves; the dummy swung forward and butted him on the nose; he said (very visibly) a wicked word, and looked guiltily out at the pair of wide blue eyes watching him. Bridie turned at once to a kindly old gentleman passing by and asked him what the word meant, pointing in at Mr Paget.

'No! No!' Mr Paget mouthed in horror, and waved his hands, but then had to lurch sideways to catch the dummy, and knocked over a chair; which was the point when Mr Rummage stormed out of the main entrance.

'Get away from that window!' he bellowed, shaking his fists. 'I will not have vagrants and costermongers on my property! I'll have the law on you! Smoking up my windows and leaving your filthy rubbish on the pavement! Get away! Go on! Hook it!'

Dippy didn't want to move, because standing in the

bright light of the window among the crowds going in and out of the shop was good for business; but Mr Rummage was a roaring, red-faced bully, and no one could stand up to his shouting for long. So the gang helped Dippy to move and set up a little further away, and Mr Rummage scowled and strutted back inside.

'Great bellowing bag of wind,' said Bridie.

'I'd like to get me *revenge* on him,' scowled Benny.

The gang had taken a dim view of Mr Rummage since the time he'd run them out of the shop for offering to demonstrate the camping equipment. It was Benny's idea. They'd offered to pitch a tent inside the store, and cook meals on a 'Vesuvius' Patent Folding Stove, and filter water with an 'Anti-buggo' Microbial Filter, and sleep in the 'Kumfi-snooze' Patent Sleeping Valise, and they'd even put on a display of Apache war dancing to entertain the customers. Benny was very proud of this plan. In the way of his plans, this one had soon spun out of control, and he imagined a Corps of Demonstrators, highly skilled and efficiently trained kids, say about ten thousand of them to start with, who'd be paid by grateful shopkeepers throughout the kingdom to show customers how to use the goods on sale. Benny would take a small percentage, say about seventy-five per cent, and within a year he'd be rich, have branches in America, float the company on the Stock Exchange, stand for Parliament, et cetera, et cetera.

Anyway, he was explaining to Mr Rummage how useful it would be when Thunderbolt had that accident with the 'Luxuriosum' Folding Umbrella Tent, and then the Peretti twins got carried away in the 'Pegasus' Self-Propelled Invalid Chair, and Sharky Bob discovered the 'Surprise' Officers' Dried Food Ration Tin, and things got out of control. Mr Rummage had thrown them all out bodily and forbidden them to enter the store ever again.

'Here, Dippy,' said Benny, 'where's me change?'

'Oh, sorry,' said Dippy. 'You give me a shilling, didn't yer? Here's a threepenny bit and a nice new tanner.'

Benny took it, but looked at it oddly and bit it.

'Here, Dippy,' he said, 'this is snide, this is. Where'd you get it from?'

He held it out. It was new and shiny, and there was Queen Victoria and all the letters around the edge, and there was a toothmark right across Her Majesty's nose.

'It's snide all right,' said Bridie. 'Look, Dippy, it ain't a proper sixpence at all!'

They all crowded close. Dippy took the coin and tested it with his four remaining teeth.

'Yeah, I reckon you're right,' he said, baffled. 'It's a fake, and no error. Wonder who passed that on me? Here, you better have some proper money.'

He didn't have another sixpence, so he gave Benny six ordinary pennies, and looked at the snide sixpence with disgust. Thunderbolt could see something else in his expression, too. A sixpence was a lot of money when you only made two or three shillings a day.

But then an old lady came along and bought some chestnuts for her granddaughter, and then Johnny

Hopkins came out of the Welsh Harp wiping his whiskers and bought some too, and the gang said goodbye to Dippy and wandered off.

'It's not fair,' Bridie said when they reached the Waxworks. 'Whoever gave Dippy that snide sixpence knew they were cheating.'

'It's not fair not letting him be a waxwork either,' Benny said. 'All them waxworks in the Museum, all they done was murder people and discover America and be Kings and Queens and that. Where's the justice in that? I bet if Dippy was a victim of the Death of a Thousand Cuts they'd put him in all right.'

'There's not enough of Dippy to make a thousand bits,' said Bridie.

Benny scowled at the closed door of the Waxwork Museum.

'We'll get Dippy in there if it's the last thing we do,' he said.

When Benny's expression was set like that, the rest of the gang knew better than to argue with him. The others left him there, frowning Napoleonically, and walked home towards Clayton Terrace.

'I wouldn't mind putting one over that Professor who owns the Waxworks,' said Bridie. 'He slung me and Sharky out last July.'

'I bet I can guess why,' said Thunderbolt.

'Well it was only a little finger off one of the blokes being tortured in the Chamber of Horrors, and he'd lost a lot more than that already. Ye'd hardly notice.'

'What did it taste like, Sharky?'

'Nice,' said Sharky Bob stolidly.

'And the Professor made us pay for it, and I had a threepenny bit, and he took it all. I bet that's enough for a whole arm.'

They walked on through the gathering mist, which was making the gaslights look like dandelion heads.

'I hope Dippy doesn't get another snide sixpence,' said Thunderbolt.

'Ma got one in the butcher's yesterday,' said Bridie. 'Ye should have heard her cursing. Hey, is that yer Pa down there?'

They were outside Number Fifteen, where Thunderbolt and his Pa lived on the ground floor and

Bridie and the rest of her large family lived upstairs. Bridie was peering down into the area, the little space in front of the basement window, where an eerie glow was flickering through the grimy window onto the damp bricks.

'Yeah,' said Thunderbolt. 'He's making something new. I dunno what it is, 'cause it's a trade secret.'

Mr Dobney was in the novelty and fancy gifts trade. He made candlesticks that looked like dragons, pipe-cleaner-dispensers that looked like dog-kennels, soda-water-bottle-holders that swivelled round on a turntable and all kinds of ingenious devices. His latest line was a combined glove-holder and dog-whistle, but for some reason there was no demand for them, and they hadn't sold at all. So he'd rented the base-ment specially and started making a new line, only Thunderbolt wasn't allowed to know what it was. All he did know was that it involved electricity: Pa had lugged a lot of heavy batteries and coils of wire down there, and occasional flashes and electrical humming sounds came out from behind the closed door.

'I better get in,' said Thunderbolt. 'Put his tea on.'

'I likes tea,' said Sharky Bob. 'I likes biscuits, and all.'

'Yeah, Sharky, we know,' said Bridie. 'What ye got for yer tea, then?'

'A couple of herrings,' said Thunderbolt.

'How ye going to cook 'em?'

'Dunno. Boil 'em, I suppose. They're only a kind of kipper, and you boil kippers.'

Bridie shook her head in exasperation. 'I better show ye.'

Thunderbolt had been looking after his Pa for nearly a year now, and Mr Dobney had never complained yet. Thunderbolt felt a bit put out by Bridie's contempt for his cooking, but he let her storm into the kitchen and bang about till she found the frying-pan. She was about to put it on the range when she recoiled, and held it under the lamplight to look more closely.

'What in the world've ye been cooking in this?' she said, picking disgustedly at some tar-like substance on the bottom.

'Toffee, I think,' said Thunderbolt, trying to

remember. 'That was when Pa thought of going into the toffee-apple trade, and he was trying to find a cheap way of making toffee. He used fish-oil instead of butter, only it didn't set properly . . .'

Bridie put down the frying-pan and found a skillet. 'This'll do,' she said. 'Give us the herrings and a knife and find me some salt.'

She slid the knife deftly up and down and scraped out some fascinating strings and blobs of fish-innards. Sharky Bob stopped licking the frying-pan and reached for them automatically, and she slapped his hand away.

'Right, now what ye do is make the skillet hot and scatter it with a big spoon of salt and lay the fishes on it. They're oily enough to sizzle by theirselves without any grease. What're ye reading?'

She laid the herrings where Sharky couldn't reach them, tucked a strand of curly red hair behind her ear, and peered at the open books on the table.

'Me homework,' Thunderbolt explained. 'We got to copy out and learn ten words out the dictionary, together with what they mean.'

'*Aardvark*,' read Bridie. '*An edentate insectivorous quadruped*. Well, that's helpful, I'm sure. *Ambergris: fatty substance of a marmoriform or striated appearance exuded from the intestines of the sperm whale, and highly esteemed by perfumiers*. Yuchh. *Asbestos: a fine fibrous amphibole of chrysotile, capable of incombustibility* . . . What in the world does all that mean?'

'Oh, we don't have to know what it means. Only what it says.'

'And that's what ye get up to in school? Catch *me* going,' said Bridie, removing the frying-pan from Sharky Bob. 'Come on, Shark, time to go. Bye, Thunderbolt.'

Thunderbolt said goodbye, stirred up the fire and put another few lumps of coal on it, brought the lamp to the table and sat down to finish his homework.

'Hello, son,' said Mr Dobney, coming in after a few minutes. 'Blooming cold down there. Brrr! What's for tea?'

He rubbed his hands and held them out to the fire.

'Herrings,' said Thunderbolt. 'I never knew they had giblets in 'em, like chickens do. Bridie took 'em out and showed me how to cook 'em proper. They'll taste all right this time.'

'Tasted all right to me last time,' said Mr Dobney, sitting in the rocking chair and unfolding the paper.

Thunderbolt loved his Pa, and he knew his Pa loved him, but neither of them would have dreamed of saying so. Instead, Mr Dobney was always nice about his son's cooking, and Thunderbolt always thought his father's latest invention would be the best of all, and there was nothing nicer than sitting by the fire of an evening with the kettle simmering and the brass Buddha gleaming on the mantelshelf and Mr Dobney reading scandal out of the paper while Thunderbolt arranged his Museum.

'See you've cleaned the old frying-pan then,' said Mr Dobney. 'Watcher got there?'

'It's a bit of lead,' said Thunderbolt. 'It came off that statue of King Neptune outside the Lamb and Flag. *You* remember.'

He took down the little brass-bound chest that belonged to his Uncle Sam the sailor, and which contained all the treasures of his Museum: the walrus tooth engraved with a picture of the *Cutty Sark* in little scratchy black lines; a dried sea-horse; several cowrie shells; a genuine bone from the nose of a cannibal chief, which Uncle Sam had won from him in a poker game; a lump of rubbery stuff from the Sargasso Sea, which Thunderbolt thought was probably a dried jellyfish. And then there were Thunderbolt's own discoveries: a halfpenny which had been run over by a tram; a twig off one of the bushes in Battersea Park, which if you held it the right way and squinted a bit looked exactly like a little old man; a broken glass slide from a magic lantern, showing Glamis Castle with what Thunderbolt *knew* was a ghost at one of the windows; and forty-six bits of old-fashioned clay pipe from the Thames mud. When they broke a clay pipe, in the olden days when they used to smoke clay pipes, there was nothing to do with it but throw it away, and most of them ended up in the river.

He laid them all out on the table and noticed that he'd spelled Sargasso wrongly on the card that belonged to the dried jellyfish. He rewrote it carefully and scraped a bit of fluff off the lump, which was looking fairly battered. It was a dull colour, sort of grey, really, with sooty streaks. Some of it came off under his fingernail, and he looked at it dubiously.

'Wossat?' said Pa. 'That's old Sam's petroleum wax, innit?'

'I thought it was a dried jellyfish,' said Thunderbolt.

'No, no, son. That's petroleum wax. He got it from Trinidad. They have this blooming great lake there made of tar. You can walk on it. Here! That's a thought! Shoes with soles made of tar – they'd be waterproof, wouldn't they? I'll have to look into that. No, that's wax, that is.'

'Wax! Dippy! The Waxworks!'

Thunderbolt jumped up excitedly. Pa looked across the top of his paper in mild astonishment, and Thunderbolt explained about Dippy's ambition.

'Ah, I get it,' said Pa, rolling the heavy lump towards him. 'Make a nice head, this would. Funny colour, mind. Still, Dippy's not a healthy colour hisself . . .'

'We could make a body for it and smuggle it in . . . *Dippy Hitchcock, World-Famous Hot-Chestnut Man.* Pity he's not a murderer really. He'd get in easy, then.'

'You wouldn't have to smuggle the whole thing in,' said Pa. 'Just the head.'

'He can't just be a head! *Dippy Hitchcock, the Famous Hot-Chestnut Disembodied Head!*'

'No, no. Just whip the bonce off Charles the Second or Admiral Nelson or someone and bung Dippy's nut up there instead.'

Thunderbolt felt doubtful. 'I dunno. I think he ought to be hisself, not masquerading as someone else. Wouldn't be the same somehow . . .'

He rolled the petroleum wax towards him. There must have been four pounds of it – maybe five. Then he saw the newspaper, which Pa had picked up again, and read a little headline off the back.

'*Fraudulent utterance of forged coins* . . . What's that, Pa? That story there.'

'Oh, that? Nothing. Lot of fuss about nothing. Come on, Samuel, put yer stuff away, it's nearly bedtime.'

His Pa had never called him Thunderbolt. In fact he'd only been Thunderbolt since the summer, when he'd knocked out Crusher Watkins from the Lower Marsh Gang. Crusher had said something about Thunderbolt's Ma, and Thunderbolt had flown at him with one colossal blow that knocked him out cold – a thunderbolt. Ever since then he'd lived in mortal dread of meeting Crusher again; but it had been worth it.

Two

Arrest

'That's *exactly* what I was going to suggest,' said Benny next day.

That wasn't quite true. What Benny had really been going to suggest was that the gang set up their own Waxwork Museum to compete with the one in the New Cut. The vision of it was already shimmering in his mind like a gigantic soap bubble: an ornate entrance, queues a mile long, waxworks so real they just about sang and danced. A Chamber of Horrors that would freeze the blood of a ghoul. In Benny's mind Kaminsky's Royal and National Waxworks expanded to fill a space roughly the size of the Crystal Palace, and it was such a success that they had to take it on a tour of America, and he came back a millionaire, and before long he was Sir Benny – Lord Kaminsky – the Duke of Lambeth . . . Were there any princesses he could marry?

But in the meantime all they had was Thunderbolt's lump of petroleum wax, or dried jellyfish, or whatever it was. They were sitting in the loft over Hodgkins's Livery Stables, surrounded by straw and the rich smell of horse, and Thunderbolt was showing them the potential head of Dippy Hitchcock.

'I reckon it's beeswax,' said Bridie.

'That ain't beeswax,' said Benny. His father was a tailor, so he knew. 'Beeswax is hard and yeller. This is petroleum wax, no error. They make candles out of it. Easy to carve, and all . . .' He was busy shaving bits off with his penknife. 'Eyes,' he said. 'What we gonna do for eyes?'

Thunderbolt held out a faded watery-looking blue marble.

'This is about the same colour as Dippy's,' he said.

'What use is one?' said Bridie. 'Though I suppose

he could be winking. Or have a patch over it like Lord Nelson.'

'I got a blood alley too,' said Thunderbolt doubtfully, fishing out a large white marble with red streaks.

'That'll do,' said Benny. 'He can have one good 'un, and the other can be bloodshot. We need summing for his whiskers, and all . . .'

Making the waxwork took the best part of a day. Benny hung around his father's workshop and borrowed a suit someone hadn't paid for, Bridie contributed a pair of her Uncle Mike's boots, and Thunderbolt managed to snip some hair off the tail of Jasper, the bad-tempered horse in the stable below.

And while Bridie and Thunderbolt stuffed the suit with straw, stuck a broomstick through for a spine and pummelled it all roughly Dippy-shaped, Benny set to work on the head.

The wax was easy to carve. He excavated two holes for eyes, and put the wax he'd dug out aside to make a nose with. Getting the eyes to look right took a long time, and still he wasn't sure it looked exactly like Dippy, not *exactly*; but then it needed a nose, after all. He reached for the wax he'd taken out, and found it was gone.

He knew where to look. Sharky Bob was licking his lips.

'It might be poison,' Benny said hopefully.

'It's nice,' said Sharky. 'I likes that.'

Benny sighed, dug a lump out of the back of the neck to make a nose with, and carried on. After an hour of squeezing the head and pulling it, of smoothing it and rubbing it and squinting at it through half-closed eyes, of trying to shove horsehair under its nose for a moustache and bits of broken china into its mouth for teeth, he reckoned it was done.

'There,' he said proudly.

The others clustered round.

'Hmm,' said Bridie. 'He looks as if he's going to puke.'

Benny shut the mouth. At once the head took on the pursed-up expression of someone who's just swallowed a caterpillar.

'He's cross-eyed,' said Thunderbolt. 'He looks as drunk as a fish.'

With a heavy sigh, Benny licked his finger and

repositioned the dots of liquorice that he'd stuck on the marbles for pupils.

'I'm still not sure about his gob-box,' said Bridie. 'Dippy's is always hanging open.'

With an even heavier sigh, Benny prised the mouth open again. Now Dippy looked like an apprehensive patient about to undergo a new and untried form of dental surgery.

'That's better,' said Thunderbolt. 'But his eyes . . . I dunno . . .'

'You do it then!' said Benny passionately. 'You're so blooming clever, you show us how his eyes ought to go! I spose you been making eyes all your life! I spose you're an *expert* on eyes! I spose no one knows *anything* about eyes except you! I spose people come from all over the *world* to ask you about eyes! Well, go on then! *You* make 'em look right, since you're the only one as knows how!'

He thrust the sticky head at Thunderbolt, who prodded and scraped and shoved for a minute or two. When he'd finished, the blue eye was gazing at the ceiling with the air of a desperate appeal for help, while the red one leered at the floor like a murderer gloating over his victim.

They all stood back and studied it critically.

'Well . . .' said Bridie.

'It ain't got a body yet, has it?' said Benny impatiently. 'Shove it on the broomstick. Course it don't look right just sitting there like a . . . like a *head*.'

Thunderbolt and Bridie waggled the head to and fro till it was well and truly jammed down on the broomstick.

'Ah!' said Benny, and Bridie said, 'That's more like it!' and Sharky Bob said, 'Cor!'

The others could only nod. It was a masterpiece.

Thunderbolt had been carefully writing a label for it, with all the words spelled correctly, and now he pinned it to the dummy's coat like a medal:

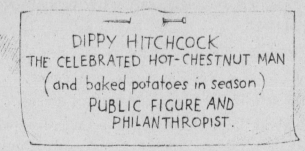

DIPPY HITCHCOCK
THE CELEBRATED HOT-CHESTNUT MAN
(and baked potatoes in season)
PUBLIC FIGURE AND
PHILANTHROPIST.

'What's that last word?' said Bridie.

'It means benefactor of mankind,' said Thunderbolt. 'I found it in the dictionary. It's real, all right.'

'Come on then,' said Benny. 'Let's get him to the Museum.'

This was the part of the whole business they'd thought about least. At the back of everyone's mind had been the vague notion that they'd just walk in, set the wax Dippy in a prime position, and walk out again without being seen. But they soon realized that it wasn't going to be that easy.

In fact, the closer they got to the Museum, the more they realized that it wasn't going to be easy at all. For one thing, it cost money to go in, and there was only enough of Benny's shilling left for two of them.

'It'll have to be me and Bridie,' said Benny. 'Sharky's too little, and Thunderbolt's too clumsy.'

It was true, and Thunderbolt had to admit it; so he and Sharky Bob stood across the road from the entrance of the Museum. It was just getting dark. The first lamps were being lit, and the shop windows on either side of the Waxworks glowed bright with their abundance of china plates and hardware, their red and green apothecary's flasks and mahogany drawers of pills. The placard inside the Museum window flickered dimly in the gruesome light shining on it. The proprietor, Professor Dupont, was too canny to put an actual waxwork there, where people could see it free.

Benny and Bridie, carrying the dummy between them with a fine display of casualness, as if it was the sort of thing that everyone took about as a matter of course and they were surprised to see no one else carrying one, dodged across the road between the carts and the omnibuses and ran up the steps to the Museum entrance. There was a little window inside the door where you paid your threepence to the grim lady dressed in black. The tickets were a different colour each day, so you couldn't save yesterday's and go in with that.

They sauntered in, with the dummy's feet bumping on the steps behind them and an inquisitive dog sniffing

in their wake. A second or two went by, and Benny and Bridie came out again, in a hurry. In fact, they were running, and no sooner had they skidded to a halt and turned back indignantly than the dummy came hurtling out after them. Bridie caught it neatly, and had to hold it up over the excited dog while Benny shook his fist at

the Professor, who took one disdainful look and shut the door.

Thunderbolt and Sharky Bob hadn't even had time to speak.

'Huh,' said Benny with profound scorn. 'Seems to me he doesn't *want* his blooming Waxworks to be successful. Seems to me he wants the same old boring Kings and Queens as every other Waxworks. He's jealous, that's what he is.'

They didn't want to stay there for too long. People were beginning to make unfunny remarks about dummies and Guy Fawkes, and three or four dogs were leaping up and trying to kill it, so the gang trooped crossly back to the stable before going their different ways home.

Thunderbolt was the last to leave. He was feeling fed up. His petroleum wax, and Benny had commandeered it to make the head; his idea in the first place, and he was too clumsy to take the dummy into the Waxworks . . . Nothing was right, somehow. The cold dim light filtering in through the filthy skylight of the stable loft didn't help, and nor did that blooming dummy propped up against a wall. Now he looked at it properly, Thunderbolt thought that he'd never seen anything so horrible.

With a shudder, Thunderbolt closed the trapdoor and climbed down into the stable, avoiding the teeth of old Jasper, to find the stable dog Jezebel whining and scratching at the bottom of the ladder.

'What is it, Jez?' he said.

Jezebel licked his hands with more than her usual friendliness, and howled mournfully. Thunderbolt hurried home through the gathering evening, keeping an eye out for Crusher Watkins and the Lower Marsh Gang.

As he passed the market, he heard Mr Ionides the costermonger shout at a baffled customer: 'Get out of it! Go and pitch yer snide somewhere else!'

More fake sixpences, Thunderbolt thought.

Then from nowhere, and for no reason at all, an idea came into his head. Supposing . . . No, he couldn't even put it into words. But the idea wouldn't go away. *Supposing it was Pa doing the coining?*

And once he'd said it to himself it was easier to go

on thinking it, though it made him feel hot and heavy, as if he was ill.

Because things had been tight recently. The 'Handi-Cheep' combined glove-holder and dog-whistle had been a failure, and Pa had put a lot into that. And no one seemed to want the self-adjusting pipe-bowl cleaner, and all the 'Eesi-Snip' Smoker's Companions had fallen apart because of a faulty hinge.

And now Pa was busy at something he refused to talk about, even though he and Thunderbolt usually shared everything.

By the time he got as far as that, Thunderbolt had stopped walking altogether. No! The idea was crazy!

(But yesterday when he'd seen the newspaper article about the forged coins, Pa had folded the paper up hastily and sent him to bed.)

His Pa would never do anything criminal!

(But Uncle Sam had stolen the little brass Buddha on the mantelshelf from a hotel in Rangoon. At least, he'd always claimed he had. And crime ran in families, everyone knew that.)

His family weren't like that.

(But hadn't he, Thunderbolt, become a receiver of stolen property? He was a criminal himself!)

He came to, miserably, outside the butcher's, and remembered what he was going to get for tea. In he went, scuffing up the sawdust, and waited while Mr Graham the butcher parcelled up a leg of pork.

'That's one and sixpence, my love. And a proper sixpence if you please, none of these fancy ones.'

'My neighbour got one in her change yesterday,' said the customer. 'Blooming wicked. How can poor folks live with rotten money going around? Why don't they forge gold sovereigns like what rich people use? Eh?'

When the customer had left, Thunderbolt said, 'A tuppenny pie, please.'

He paid for the pie, and when it was wrapped he said, 'Are there lots of these snide coins about, Mr Graham?'

'They're turning up all over the place, son. All over Lambeth, anyway. *And* shillings and half-crowns. There must be a whole gang of smashers going round.'

Smashers were the people who actually passed fake coins into circulation. Thunderbolt's heart lifted: Pa wasn't part of a gang, that was certain.

'So one person on their own, like, they couldn't be doing it?'

'One person could be *making* 'em,' said Mr Graham. 'Old Stamper Billings used to work on his own, and he kept going for years.'

'Who?'

'Stamper Billings. *You* remember him, Arthur!' said Mr Graham to a thin old man who'd just come in.

'Old Stamper, yeah, I remember him,' wheezed the old man. 'He turned out all kinds, old Stamper. Course, they caught him in the end – the year Sefton won the Derby. He had a regular crew of smashers. They used to come down from the West End, Soho, and from East as far as Limehouse. That's where he was clever, see. He never uttered 'em round here, so folks was less inclined to peach on him. There's always a nose near by; you don't last long in that trade. But old Stamper lasted longer'n most.'

'Uttered means passed,' said Mr Graham. 'That's

the legal term for it. They got him for uttering.'

'Have you taken any of the snide ones, Mr Graham?' said Thunderbolt.

'Yeah, worse luck. D'you want 'em? They're no good to me.'

The butcher fished into the pocket of his apron and brought out three coins.

'Don't you try to spend 'em, now,' he said.

'No! I don't want to spend them. I'm going to put them in my Museum.'

Thunderbolt took the pie to the bakery to be heated. He could think of nothing but the forged coins, and when the pie was in the oven he asked Mr Solomons the baker if *he'd* taken any counterfeit coins.

'No, I'm too fly,' said Mr Solomons. 'They won't get any of them things past me.'

'What do they do to forgers when they catch them?'

'They hang 'em, me boy. It's a capital crime, defacing Her Majesty the Queen. Making false coins is as bad as treason.'

Thunderbolt gulped. 'Do you know how they

make fake coins, Mr Solomons?'

The baker looked around, saw there was no one near by, and leaned over the floury wooden counter of the shop to speak confidentially.

'I heard,' he said, 'from a cousin of mine who's a policeman, that they make a plaster-of-Paris mould off a real new coin, and melt some cheap metal and pour it in. Then to make it look like silver they get a bath of spirits of salt and cyanide, 'cause that's got silver in it, and dip the coins in that and pass an electric current through with a wire from a battery. That makes a bit of silver stick to the coin. There's a craft in it, see.'

Thunderbolt could hardly hear; there was a kind of roaring in his ears. Those electric batteries in the cellar – that wire . . .

He took the fragrant steaming pie when it was ready and hurried across the road towards home. Then he slowed down. He hurried again; he came to a halt; he didn't know whether to run or stand still.

Finally, heavily, he dragged his steps in through the front door. There was a glow from the area window, like yesterday. And that sharp faint smell: was that spirits of salt? What did they smell like? What *were* spirits of salt?

Thunderbolt took the pie into the kitchen and lit the lamp.

Then he thought: I *must* go and see what he's doing.

He went out into the scullery at the back, where there was a dark little staircase that led down.

And when he got to the bottom of the stairs, he heard voices. Pa was talking to someone.

'I should take 'em up West,' he was saying. 'Try Oxford Street. Lambeth's no good any more. Or you could try up Whiteley's in Queensway . . .'

The other voice said something, and then the outer door closed. Then there were the sounds of tools being put away, and a swishing sound as his father swept the floor, whistling heartlessly. Thunderbolt crept up the stairs again and washed his hands under the pump in the yard, and splashed some water on his face, too, in case his eyes were red.

He stoked the range and put the pie on the table, but that was as far as he got towards making the tea;

because just then, as his father came along the hall, there was a loud banging at the front door.

Thunderbolt's heart leaped with fear. He heard Pa's footsteps halt and then turn towards the door; he heard the handle turn; he heard a loud official voice say:

'Frederick William Dobney?'

'Yus, that's me,' said Pa mildly.

'Frederick William Dobney, I am arresting you on the charge of—'

'NO!'

Thunderbolt flung the kitchen door open and hurled himself down the hall. There was a fat policeman at the door, with a thin one beside him, and there was Pa, looking baffled. The thin policeman made a grab for Thunderbolt before he got to Pa, and held him back. He was too strong. As hard as Thunderbolt struggled, he couldn't break free.

'Pa! Pa!' he shouted desperately, but the other policeman had the handcuffs on his father already, and Pa couldn't move.

'Let me talk to my boy!' Pa was saying, but the fat policeman wouldn't, so Pa shouted, 'Let go! Let me talk

to him! You can't take me away like this — what's *he*
going to do? Sam! Sammy! Don't . . .'

But Thunderbolt didn't hear any more, because the
fat policeman was bundling Pa into a closed wagon, and
the driver was shaking the reins. Thunderbolt watched
with helpless horror as the police wagon trundled away,
taking his father with it.

Then there came a great roaring Irish voice from behind, and the clatter of a dozen pairs of feet on the stairs.

'What the devil are ye holding the boy for, ye whey-faced beanstick? Let him go this minute, or I'll take yer helmet and ram it up yer nose!'

Mrs Malone bore down on the policeman like a force of nature. Lightning seemed to play around her head. The policeman took a deep breath to try and speak in his defence, and in the same moment Thunderbolt twisted out of his grasp and hurled himself down the steps into the road, and away.

Three

Into Action

'Thunderbolt?'

Bridie's head looked up through the trapdoor. She called again, softly, and held the little candle-lantern higher.

'Ah, there ye are . . .'

He lay curled up in the furthest corner. His eyes were closed. She clambered in and shut the trap behind her.

'Hey! Wake up, look, I've brought yer pie. Ye must be famished.'

She set the lantern down on an upturned orange-box and unfolded the dirty cloth she'd carried the pie in. Thunderbolt was still pretending to be asleep, and shivering with cold, the poor spalpeen, she thought.

She nudged him with her foot.

'Hey! Thunderbolt! It's only me. The coppers have all gone. Wake up, ye old fool.'

Thunderbolt yawned and pretended to wake up elaborately. He fumbled for his glasses and put them on before opening his eyes.

'Oh. Wotcher, Bridie . . .'

'I brought yer pie.'

'That was for Pa's tea.'

'They'll give him some nosh where he's gone. Eat up or I will.'

'Share it then.'

She cut it in two with her pocket knife and gave him the larger piece.

'What did they nab him for?' she asked.

'Counterfeiting,' he said. In fact he didn't say it clearly at all; his voice shook and she could hardly hear him. Then she worked out what he'd said.

'Ye mean coining? They think *he's* doing it? Begod! That's crazy!'

She laughed loudly enough to make Jasper shift his feet down below. Thunderbolt said nothing; he sat looking down, stolidly chewing the pie.

'Listen, Thunderbolt,' she said, shaking his arm, 'they'll have to let yer Pa go as soon as they find out he never done it. It's a mistake! Yer Pa's no snide-pitcher. Anyway, ye can't stay here. Supposing they lets him out, and he goes home and finds ye gone, and the fire's out and there's no food or nothing?'

Then it was his turn to shrug. And something in the hopeless, unhappy look of him made her suddenly understand why he'd run away.

'Well, anyway,' she said after a moment, 'pile the hay over ye, that'll keep ye warm. I won't leave the lantern, 'cause ye're a clumsy divil at the best of times and ye'd set the place alight. Ye've got old Dippy there for company – he's better than a watch-dog, if ye ask me. One squint at him and the boldest murderer'd take to his heels. And ye've got half a pie inside ye, so ye won't starve till breakfast time. Go to sleep now, and I'll bring ye a can of milk in the morning.'

'You won't tell anyone I'm here?' he muttered.

'Ye mean Ma? Sure I won't. If she knew where ye were she'd have ye out by the ear and upstairs with us lot in half a shake. Ye're better off out of it. But I'll tell Benny and the others. This is a gang matter now.'

Next morning was cold and damp. The gang should have been at school, but most of them regarded the School Board as the slow-witted opponent in a delightful game, and played hookey at the slightest opportunity. Bridie intercepted Benny on his way out of his father's tailor's shop.

He was outraged when he heard what had happened. Bridie had to thump him before he'd calm down and listen.

'Will ye stow yer noise! Of course the man's innocent and someone else is passing the fakes, but Thunderbolt thinks his father's *guilty*!'

Benny stopped at once. They were on the corner of Crowquill Walk and Hopton Street, at the edge of Lower Marsh territory, and Crusher Watkins and two of his pals were ambling along schoolwards on the other side of the road. They yelled out some coarse remark, but Benny didn't even hear it.

'He *what?*'

'I could tell. 'Cause Mr Dobney *could* be the forger, see. He's got all the right bits and pieces in that basement, and he knows all about metalwork and so on.'

'I don't believe it,' said Benny. 'And nor should Thunderbolt. Let's go and—'

'There's no point in saying what he should or shouldn't believe,' Bridie said impatiently. 'Poor feller, he's only got his Pa. He thinks the world of his Pa. If he can't trust him any more . . .'

Benny was a passionate, generous boy, and he saw what Bridie meant.

'Right,' he said. 'Right, I'm angry now. We gotta get some *justice*. We gotta do some *detecting*.'

Only the previous summer, Benny had done a job for Mr Sexton Blake, the great detective. It had only been a matter of taking a message to someone and bringing back the reply, but Mr Blake had given him half a crown and told him he was a sharp lad. For the next two weeks, the gang made life a misery for every adult in the New Cut, detecting like frenzy; until they saw the Texas Cowboy Lasso Artists at the Music Hall, anyway, and took to rope-twirling instead. But that detecting had been kids' stuff. This was real.

'First go off,' said Benny, 'we'll go and see Dippy . . .'

They tracked him down at the market, where he was buying a sack of chestnuts.

'How'd you get on at the Waxworks? Am I on display yet?' he said.

'Not quite,' said Benny. 'Listen, Dippy – you still got that snide sixpence?'

'Yeah. Got it here somewhere . . .' The old man fumbled in his waistcoat pocket.

'I'll give yer a ha'penny for it,' said Benny. 'This is evidence, this is.'

The old man was pleased to make something out of the deal, and then the costermonger near by said, 'I've got one, and all. Want to buy that?'

Before long Benny had two more snide sixpences and a snide shilling, and then he ran out of money to buy them with.

'When they catch the geezer as done 'em,' the costermonger said, 'they oughter chop his head orf. Taking money out of people's mouths! If it was good enough for Charles the First, it'd be good enough for him.'

'We'll see about that,' said Benny.

Half an hour later, the whole gang was sitting around the orange-box in the stable loft. Bridie had brought a can of milk for Thunderbolt, as she'd promised, and Benny contributed a bagel, and Sharky Bob offered a second-hand humbug, which was so extraordinarily generous that Thunderbolt felt he had to accept.

'Right,' said Benny. 'First we got to examine the evidence.'

He hauled out the coins he'd acquired, which had become jumbled up in his pocket with the rest of the debris there: a piece of chalk, a magnet with several nails stuck to it, a box of Lucifer matches, another box containing a peculiar worm which hadn't moved for several days, a genuine Jezail bullet, a bit of mirror with the edges bound with sticky tape for looking round corners with, a badly scratched lens for examining footprints and bloodstains and lighting fires, and a ragged handkerchief the colour of mud.

He laid the coins out in a row – all shiny, all extremely real-looking, and each of them somewhere marked with a tooth-bite, showing that they were made of soft metal and not proper silver.

'The first clue,' he said, 'is that they all come from round here. From Dippy and the market, mostly.'

'And I got some from the butcher,' said Thunderbolt. He said it without thinking, and then realized that he might be incriminating his father, but it was too late. 'He told me about Stamper Billings.'

'Who?' said Bridie.

'He was a snide-pitcher,' said Thunderbolt. 'He lived round the New Cut a long time ago.'

'His stuff might be around somewhere still,' said Benny. 'His tools and that. We oughter find out where he lived. And then we oughter find out where these 'uns are being put in circulation. We know there's a lot round here, but is there any round Lower Marsh? Or further off like the Elephant and Castle or Lambeth

Walk? 'Cause they might not be coming from here at all. So what we gotta do is spread out all round Lambeth and find out where there's been snide coins uttered. Only don't say uttered. There's no point using words if you have to explain what they mean each time you say 'em. Just find out how far it goes, and then come back and we'll work out where the centre of it all is.'

'Then what?' said Bridie.

'Then we'll *know*, of course! And we'll be able to clear Thunderbolt's Pa.'

Thunderbolt had become very red. He looked down at the dusty floor and poked a wisp of straw through a crack in the boards.

'Right,' said Bridie. 'We'll do that. Me and Sharky'll go down the Elephant.'

'I likes Elephant,' said Sharky Bob.

'You ain't never ate an elephant!' said Bridie.

'I bet he could,' said Benny. 'And we'll get the rest of the gang to help, and all. We'll get the Peretti twins and—'

'No!' said Thunderbolt desperately.

Bridie shook her head, and Benny said, 'No, maybe

not. So you and Sharky's going down the Elephant, and I'll do up Waterloo. And Thunderbolt can do round Lime Tree Walk, and we'll all meet back here at four o'clock . . .'

He and Bridie and Sharky Bob swarmed down the ladder and hurried off in their different directions. Thunderbolt went more slowly. He was reluctant to go into the street, because he felt that everyone who looked at him would know that he was the son of a felon. And such a mean felony! If it had been a grand, swash-buckling felony, like piracy on the high seas, it wouldn't have been so bad. But counterfeiting six-pences was a low, sneaking, snivelling sort of crime, and it only hurt poor people, too. Thunderbolt felt bleak with misery.

And when he tried to stop thinking about Pa, the only other thing that came to mind was his lump of stolen lead, and that only made him imagine that every policeman he saw was after him personally. The lump of lead expanded in his mind to the size of the Rock of Gibraltar, and it was all covered in flags and posters saying, 'Thunderbolt did it! This way! Clayton

Terrace, Number Fifteen! The criminal Dobneys again!'

So he did his detecting glumly, and when he met the others back in the New Cut as the lamps were being lit, he felt entirely worthless.

But Bridie was carrying a couple of bags of Dippy's chestnuts, and Benny had a big stone jug of ginger beer, and Sharky Bob was clutching a bag of apples, and they all looked so full of glee that he began to cheer up. Seeing Benny eating one of the apples, he began to feel hungry too.

But before he could say anything, Benny suddenly pointed down the street and said, 'Wuph! Thumwhun's thtealing Dthippy!'

Wiping apple off his glasses, Thunderbolt looked where Benny was pointing. Someone – a little skinny man in a rat-catcher's cap – was sneaking out of the stableyard gate, and trying unsuccessfully to conceal what he was carrying: the waxwork dummy, Benny's masterpiece, the portrait of Dippy Hitchcock.

'Oi! Stop thief! Come back!'

The little man looked over his shoulder in alarm.

Seeing four determined children charging towards him, he gave a yelp and tried to run. But the dummy's dangling legs got between his feet and tripped him up, and as he rolled over on the muddy pavement, squealing with panic, the dummy's flailing arms wrapped themselves around him, so that it looked as if he were being attacked by a monster from a nightmare.

Passers-by stopped to gape. Hearing the shouts, people looked across from the market stalls, came to the door of the Rose and Crown, opened windows and stared. A group of idle layabout dogs appeared from nowhere to surround the thief and the dummy, barking with joy, just like children round a fight in the playground. An elderly cab-horse shied nervously.

The little man struggled free just as the gang arrived, scrambled to his feet, and fled. Benny was all for chasing him and making a citizen's arrest, but Bridie held him back.

'Never mind him,' she said, 'we still got the dummy.'

'Not all of it,' said Thunderbolt, lifting it up out of reach of the dogs. At some stage its nose had come off, and a terrier called Ron was eating it gleefully. When they realized what he'd got, the other dogs wanted some too, and Ron took the nose and fled; and less than a minute after it had started, all the excitement was over. Carrying the dummy between them, the gang went back into the stable yard, indignant at the dishonesty of adults.

'Shockin',' said Bridie. 'I'm really disturbed.'

'Oughter hang him, at least,' said Benny.

'You can't trust anyone.'

He tenderly removed the dummy's head, smoothing over the edges where the nose had come off, shoving the blood-alley back into its socket, removing bits of grit and mud from the cheeks.

'He musta been one of these art thieves,' he said. 'They pinch pictures and statues and fancy china and stuff. Then they flog it to museums or rich Americans. Bound to be an art thief.'

Bridie was last in. She was watching the curious behaviour of a foreign-looking man who'd seen the escape of the thief and the rescue of the dummy. He was peering closely at the ground where the thief had fallen over, and bending down to pick up something too small to see before putting it in an envelope and tucking it securely in his waistcoat pocket.

H'mm, she thought, and followed the others in.

'He looks better without his hooter,' she said, examining the damage. 'More friendly.'

'What you talking about?' said Benny. 'He looks horrible. He looks as if he's been attacked by a lion. How'd you like it if your nose was et off?'

'It wasn't a lion, anyway, it was only old Ron from the fish shop,' said Thunderbolt. 'He don't look too bad. Dig a lump out the back of his neck to make another schnozz and cover the hole with his cap. He's just a bit dusty, that's all.'

Slightly repaired, the dummy was propped up in his usual spot near the skylight, and the gang settled down around the orange-box. The candle-lantern glowed on the apples and the chestnuts as they were divided and devoured, as the ginger beer went the rounds and was emptied, and then Bridie gave Sharky a giant humbug to keep him quiet, and they began to report.

'I went up Blackfriars Bridge way and across the river,' Thunderbolt said. 'There's hardly any over the other side, but lots on this. And then I went down Lime Tree Walk and I got talking to this old beggarman, and he told me about snide-pitching. It's not making the coins that's hard – it's passing them out. He said you need lots of people, 'cause one bloke can't go into a shop or a pub with a bag full of new coins, it'd look suspicious. So they buy the tanners and shillings for a penny each, and go off and pass 'em out in lots of different places. He gave me a tanner what he'd been given. He thought there was some snide-pitching going on, 'cause normally he only gets ha'pence and farthings.'

He found his voice getting quieter and quieter. He wanted to help the gang in their detecting, but he might only be helping convict his father. What he really wanted to do was shut his eyes and hide in the dark for ever.

But Bridie was impatient to talk.

'They been getting snide coins down St George's Road and London Road,' she said, 'and one or two at the Elephant, but none down Newington Butts. Nor the New Kent Road. Nor Walworth Road.'

'D'you get any?' said Benny.

'We got three.' She tipped them out of her sticky hand and into Benny's. He looked at them closely before putting them with the rest on the orange-box. '*And*,' she went on triumphantly, 'we talked to Snake-Eyes Melmott the bookie, and he told us where Stamper Billings lived! Guess what? He lived just off the Cut, under where Rummage's is now!'

'Under it?' said Thunderbolt.

'He had a basement. Most coiners work on the top floor of a house, Snake-Eyes told us, 'cause then they can hear the coppers coming and they got time to sling everything in the fire. But Stamper worked in a basement in a row of houses where Rummage's Emporium is. Old Rummage bought up the whole row.'

Thunderbolt was listening as if his life depended on it. If most coiners worked on the top floor . . . And Pa was working in the basement . . . But Stamper Billings had worked in a basement, after all.

Benny, meanwhile, could hardly sit still. He was bursting to tell them what he'd found out.

'I've been to Grover and Cohen's in Peacock Alley,' he said. 'Them detectives — *you* remember.'

Grover and Cohen were two extremely dingy private detectives (not in the Sexton Blake class by any means) for whom Benny did occasional jobs. It turned out that he'd spent the afternoon with them, learning about snide-pitching in general and this outbreak in particular.

'But they didn't know much,' he said. 'Course, I had

to promise to do a job for 'em. They got to find an old lady's cat what's done a bunk. But I know where to find plenty of cats, that won't take long. Oh, and I got half a dozen snideys this morning down Lambeth Walk.'

He fished them out and put them with the others on the orange-box. He was fizzing and twitching with excitement, so Thunderbolt knew that something else was coming.

'And,' Benny said, 'I solved the crime!'

They looked at him blankly.

'It's true! I solved it!'

He couldn't restrain himself from getting up and doing a little jig like Paddy Phelan the Spoon Dancer. Sharky Bob joined in, shouting with glee.

'He's got a mouse in his drawers,' said Bridie. Then she hit him. 'Stow it, ye half-wit! Sit down and tell us, if ye're such a Sexton Blake!'

So Benny stopped and said, 'All right. All right. When did Stamper Billings get caught?'

'Ages ago!' said Bridie.

'It was the year – the year . . .' Thunderbolt hit his

head, trying to remember what the butcher had said. 'It was the year Sefton won the Derby!'

'1878,' said Bridie at once.

'Look at the coins!' said Benny. 'Look at the date on 'em!'

A moment's stillness, and then three hands reached out to the pile of shiny silver coins.

'1878!'

'*All* of 'em?'

'It's true!'

'They are! They're all Stamper's!'

'It wasn't Thunderbolt's Pa at all!'

'But . . .'

The *but* was Thunderbolt's, and then he began to believe it. Feverishly he turned all the coins over, and they all looked new, and they all had the date 1878 firmly in the right place. He felt a great bubble of joy rising in his chest, and it nearly became a sob, but he made it into a hiccup, and turned the coins over and over, letting them fall from one hand to the other like dazzling water.

'We can prove he's innocent now!' Benny was saying.

For a moment the others clapped and cheered; but then Bridie said, 'No we can't,' and they fell quiet. She went on, 'This doesn't *prove* anything about Mr Dobney, does it? All it proves is that whoever made 'em used a new 1878 coin to make his mould from.'

'But who'd do that, in 1894?' said Thunderbolt desperately. '1878 coins is sixteen years old. They're bound to be worn a bit. These 'uns *must've* been made back then.'

'And anyway, if Stamper Billings did make 'em, why've they only started turning up now?' said Bridie.

''Cause where did Stamper live?' Benny demanded. 'Under Rummage's, that's where! What I reckon is, Stamper made hundreds of these snideys, and hid 'em, and they was never found. Then Rummage bought the place and turned it into a big shop, and found the loot in the basement or in a secret hole in the wall or summing. And it's been *him* passing 'em out.'

'But Mr Rummage is rich,' said Thunderbolt. 'What'd he want to pass out snide tanners for?'

''Cause he's mean as well as rich,' said Benny. 'We *know* he is. And he's got the perfect place to do it! In a big shop like that, what's always busy, it'd be dead easy to slip a dodgy tanner in someone's change. And we know that Rummage's is dead plum smack in the middle of the area they're going round in. The further from Rummage's, the less there are. We just proved that today.'

'It could be . . .' said Bridie. 'And the first time *we* saw one it was just outside Rummage's. I bet someone had just got it in their change and paid Dippy with it.'

'*And* they opened that new department in Rummage's basement last month!' Thunderbolt remembered. 'He could have found Stamper's coins when they did the alterations.'

'*And* he's a scurvy miserable old git,' said Benny. 'It's bound to be him.'

Mr Rummage certainly *was* a scurvy miserable old git. He was famous for it. The gang had been excluded from the Emporium after that unfortunate business in the Camping Department, but Mr Rummage didn't only exclude helpful people like them; he excluded all sorts, grown-ups as well. He got the taste for it soon after he had an electric lift fitted in the shop, one of the first in London. He had an attendant standing by on each floor with smelling salts and brandy in case the customers felt faint after this new experience. Naturally the lifts were soon crowded with customers pretending to stagger out fainting, and Mr Rummage lost his temper and excluded them. Then there was old Molly Tomkins. She was mad, but perfectly harmless. She fell in love with one of the window dummies and wanted to climb in the window to be with him. The poor old soul thought Mr Rummage had taken him prisoner. She was excluded even from walking up and down the pavement outside the window, and she used to stand across the road and signal to the dummy until they came to take her away to Bedlam.

So Rummage was a bad-tempered bully; and now he was passing out snide coins as well, or so it seemed. Thunderbolt thought of his Pa, locked in a cell. He could almost feel his thoughts beating at the prison bars like a carrier pigeon with a message of hope.

'We'll have to *get* him!' Benny said. 'We'll have to catch him red-handed.'

'But how?' said Bridie. 'He won't let us in the shop! Why don't we just go and tell the police?'

It seemed the obvious thing to do, but Thunderbolt felt a drizzle of fear at the very thought. He'd forgotten about his *own* crime for a few moments.

'Maybe,' he said wildly, 'maybe we ought to get in the shop and find the hiding-place.'

'That wouldn't take long, would it?' said Bridie. 'There's only twenty-two departments, after all. And only about ten thousand places to hide things in each one. We could probably do it in about ten minutes.'

'Well—' Thunderbolt began, but Benny held up his hand and said, 'Sssh.'

They all fell still.

Benny tiptoed over to the trapdoor and crouched to listen. Then he looked up. 'There's someone down there,' he whispered.

A spy!

They looked at one another, with a nameless thrill shivering its way up their backs. Silently each of them picked up a weapon – a catapult, a bit of stick, a clasp knife, anything that came to hand – and resolved to sell themselves dearly.

Jasper was moving about restlessly below. And then into the stillness came a creak. It was a familiar creak: it was the sound the fifteenth rung of the ladder made. The intruder was nearly at the top.

Thunderbolt, Bridie and Benny tiptoed in utter silence to the trapdoor. Sharky Bob scowled fiercely from the orange-box. A draught from somewhere made the flame in the little lantern quiver, and the shadows flapped around the loft like great dark flags.

Beneath the trapdoor they could hear a scratching, scrabbling sound as the intruder fumbled for the bolt.

He was muttering, too, and in a foreign language. Thunderbolt thought it might be French. He made out the words, '*Morbleu! Que diable ont-ils fait avec le ... Ah! Voilà ...*'

The bolt slid open.

The trapdoor lifted.

And there in the guttering lantern-light was the face of a stranger. He had a little pointed beard and a neat pearl-grey hat and kid gloves, and whatever he expected to see, it wasn't a ring of fierce faces glaring down, an array of dangerous weapons all pointed at him. He gave a startled gasp.

'*Non! Non! Aah*—'

The fifteenth step could cope with the kids' weight, but the Frenchman was plump and well-fed, and when he suddenly stepped down on to the cracked rung it gave way completely.

'*Waaaah!*' he cried as he vanished.

That's the same in French as it is in English, Thunderbolt thought, interested.

The kids all crowded to the rim of the hole and peered through. They knew it wouldn't have pleased old Jasper to have Frenchmen falling among his feet like hailstones, and a shrill whinny and a loud stamping confirmed it. More shouts of alarm in a mixture of French and panic followed, and then the spy found the stable door and fled.

The gang looked at one another. Benny shook his head.

'An escaped lunatic,' he said. 'I spect they'll catch him soon. Or maybe he was another art thief . . . Yeah, he looked like an art thief. Bound to be. But never mind him. *I* know how to catch Rummage red-handed. Close the lid and I'll tell you my plan . . .'

Four

The Transformation of Dippy Hitchcock

'Slummin',' said Benny sagely, once they were all seated round the orange-box again. 'We gotta get Rummage slummin'.'

'Eh?' said Bridie.

'Slummin'. Grover and Cohen told me about it. See, the trouble with snide coins is they look too new. If they was *real* silver tanners they'd look more battered. So he's gotta think that passing 'em out like this is dangerous, and he oughter make 'em look older by slummin' 'em. You make up a mixture of lampblack and oil and rub it in, and there they are, slummed. See? So he gets the idea that he's gotta do this, and so he does it, and we goes in and catches him red-handed.'

'Oh,' said Thunderbolt.

'I see,' said Bridie.

'How we going to make him do it in the first place?' said Thunderbolt.

'We get Dippy to go in and talk about it so Rummage overhears.'

'Dippy's been excluded,' Bridie pointed out.

'All right, someone else then! Grover or Cohen or someone. Or your uncles,' he said to Bridie.

'Well, yes, but how are *we* going to get in?' she said.

'And how are we going to prove it?' said Thunderbolt.

'I'll borrow Grover and Cohen's detective camera and take a pitcher of him doing it.'

Bridie looked doubtful.

'They won't—' said Bridie.

'Sposing—' said Thunderbolt.

'I don't think—' said Bridie.

'What if—' said Thunderbolt.

Benny lost his temper.

'You don't *deserve* me!' he stormed. 'You deserve

someone like Crusher Watkins tellin' you what to do! You deserve that bloomin' *dummy* leadin' you! I'm *wasted* here. You got no more daring nor imagination than a cupboard full of beetles! This is a plan what even Sexton Blake'd be proud of. In fact I think I'll go and work for him full time, stead of leadin' you. I think I'll be his partner. I think he'd appreciate me. He'd say he wished *he* could think of plans like that. *Yes but! Sposing! What if!*'

'I was just going to say,' said Thunderbolt, 'what if we got Dippy to let us in?'

There was a silence. Thunderbolt was sitting forward and blinking hard, the way he did when he was thinking, and he dabbed up his spectacles and tried to explain the idea that was wobbling in his mind like a soap-bubble.

'It's my lead,' he said breathlessly, 'my bit of lead what I bought from Harry Fitchett, what came off the statue on the horse-trough – and it was Dippy wanting to be a waxwork – and it was the man in the window, that other day, when Dippy got his first snide tanner—'

'What you *talking* about?' said Benny.

Thunderbolt explained. The summer before, the Metropolitan Horse-Trough and Drinking Fountain Association had made the mistake of setting up a fine lead statue of King Neptune by the horse-trough just across the road from J. Beazley the scrap-metal dealer's. This was too tempting for the local citizens to resist, with lead fetching the price it did, and thirty-six hours after the statue was unveiled it had vanished for good. Unrecognizable lumps of lead kept turning up at Beazley's yard for weeks afterwards; in fact it was one of those very lumps which was causing Thunderbolt such spasms of criminal guilt.

But once the plinth was empty, the drinkers at the Lamb and Flag nearby felt it needed occupying, so one warm evening they each got up in turn and posed for the admiration and criticism of the general public. Tommy Glossop's Napoleon had been highly praised, and Mrs Amelia Price's Lady Macbeth had pleased the connoisseurs of the drama; but Dippy Hitchcock's Moses Parting the Red Sea had drawn gasps of admiration and a round of applause. Dippy had struck a dramatic attitude and held it for so long that you'd have thought the rest of him was made of wood as well as his head, as Mrs Fanny Blodgett of the Excelsior Coffee Rooms put it. The Peretti twins had won two shillings betting on him.

'Ahh!' said Benny, with a sigh of profound satisfaction. 'I'm beginning to get it.'

'Well, tell *me* then!' said Bridie.

'We get Dippy dressed posh,' said Thunderbolt, 'and clean him up a bit, and he goes and stands in the window like a dummy till closing time, and then he lets us in.'

Bridie began to grin. Benny was grinning.

'It's a stunner!' he said. 'It's a corker!'

'It's the best one yet!' said Bridie.

And Thunderbolt began to think that things might not be so bad after all. They agreed to catch Dippy and put the plan into action next day; no point in hanging around, as Bridie said.

When they left the hideout, Thunderbolt lingered behind. Bridie said, 'Come on home, Thunderbolt.'

He twisted his lip. 'I dunno,' he said.

'We're on the right track now! Ye can sleep in yer own bed, and Ma'll give ye a feed – you can't stay here another night.'

'Well . . .'

He looked back at the dummy. It looked so forlorn and abandoned that he felt almost bound to stay and keep it company.

Bridie saw where he was looking.

'Yeah,' she said, 'I got a funny feeling about that. I reckon we ought to hide it. That thief knew where it was, and I reckon the Frenchman was after it as well, and he knows where to come now.'

'The escaped lunatic? He won't come back after a trampling from Jasper.'

'All the same, I reckon we oughter take it with us. Ye never know.'

'You never know,' said Sharky solemnly.

So they covered the wax head with an old nosebag of Jasper's, crammed the floppy limbs together and bound them tightly with a bit of twine that Thunderbolt kept round his waist as an emergency belt or climbing rope or lasso, and then manoeuvred the unwieldy bundle through the trapdoor and down the ladder, home-wards.

It was strange being home again. And not at all nice; the grate was cold and full of ash, there was no oil for the lamp, and only a bit of stale bread to eat. Thunderbolt was on the point of feeling very sorry for himself indeed when Bridie came down and invited him upstairs.

'Ma says if ye don't come and have a bite of supper she'll box yer ears,' she told him, so he had no choice.

The Malones' kitchen was full of five different kinds of noise and three different kinds of smoke. Mrs Malone was shouting, Sharky Bob was banging two spoons together, Uncle Paddy was playing a tin whistle, Mary and the two middle girls were arguing over a board game called Wibbly Wob, and a frying-pan of potatoes was hissing and bubbling on the range. The three kinds of smoke came from the frying-pan, the fire and Uncle Mikey's pipe.

'Here's the champion!' said Uncle Paddy, who'd seen the famous fight with Crusher Watkins.

'Have they let yer Da out yet?' said Mary.

'Course they haven't, else he'd've come home, wouldn't he?' snapped Bridie.

Mrs Malone turned her broad scarlet face to Thunderbolt.

'What d'ye think ye're doing skulking in a stable all night, gossoon?' she roared.

'I thought they'd arrest me as well,' Thunderbolt explained.

'Let 'em try!' she bellowed. 'Bridie! Dishes!'

She brought the frying-pan to the table, and a tide of Malones came in: from the floor, from under chairs, from under the table itself. The smaller ones perched on the big ones' knees, the uncles had a couple apiece, and

MUNCH

MUNC

Thunderbolt shared his chair with Sharky Bob.

'Mind yer bacon with Sharky!' said someone. 'Gobble it quick else he'll have it.'

Mrs Malone dished out the fried potatoes, and Uncle Paddy cut slices off a vast slab of boiled bacon. For a short while they all stopped talking. The only sound was the clatter of cutlery and the munching of a dozen full mouths.

Then there was a satisfied sigh, and then another, and Uncle Paddy said, 'That was a fine piece of bacon, Michael.'

'A happy pig, Patrick,' said Uncle Mikey, and Thunderbolt saw a secret wink pass between them.

Mrs Malone cleared the bacon away and sliced up some bread and treacle for everyone, and then Bridie

washed the dishes. Thunderbolt wondered when she was going to broach the subject of Benny's plan, but she knew her uncles; she waited until they'd got their pipes going and the kids were playing around their feet.

When she'd done the dishes she said, 'Uncle Mikey? Can ye do us a favour?'

Uncle Mikey didn't live there; he was visiting from Limehouse, where his barque was unloading.

'As long as it's tomorrow. We're back off to the Baltic Sea the day after. What d'ye want me to do?'

'You and Uncle Paddy both. Ye've got to go into Rummage's and walk around till you see Mr Rummage himself. Then ye've got to mention snide money and see if he pricks up his ears. If he comes close and listens, ye've got to talk about slummin'.'

'What the divil's that, then?' said Uncle Paddy.

'Hush, Patrick; this is a prime lark,' said Uncle Mikey. 'Carry on, girl.'

'One of ye's got to tell the other that what professionals do with new snide coins is to rub a mixture of lampblack and oil into 'em to make 'em look used. Otherwise they look too new and people get suspicious. Just make sure old Rummage hears that and then walk away casual-like. See?'

Uncle Mikey raised his ginger eyebrows and directed a long stream of smoke at the ceiling.

'I can't imagine what this is all about, but I wouldn't mind playing a trick on that great swaggering gomus,' he said. 'What d'ye say, Paddy?'

'Well, why not?' said Uncle Patrick.

And Thunderbolt felt as pleased as if both uncles belonged to him.

Next morning he intended to find Dippy at once, but unfortunately the school attendance officer was standing in the street with his little black notebook, and there was no escaping him. At playtime, Thunderbolt had a brief and almost absent-minded fight with a boy who said that Mr Dobney would certainly be hanged, and then Thunderbolt would have to go to the orphanage; and once he'd successfully mended his glasses with a piece of string from his emergency lasso, he settled down resignedly to learning the principal rivers of England and Wales. The drone of the master – the sniffing and scratching and fidgeting of the other kids – the stuffy fug that always developed when a lot of dirty bodies shared a closed space with a big iron stove – it all enveloped him with gloom.

As he trudged out of the BOYS gateway at four o'clock, he heard Benny yell 'Thunderbolt!' from across the street and saw him jumping up and down with impatience, beckoning him frantically.

He darted across.

'They done it!' Benny said. 'Bridie's uncles! They went in looking like a pair of swells, and they waited till Rummage was *this* far away, and when they started talking about snide money he jumped so much he nearly snapped his suspenders!'

Thunderbolt's gloom began to lift. 'The trouble is I ain't had time to find Dippy,' he said. 'The attendance officer nabbed us and I couldn't escape.'

'Oh, blimey. He could be anywhere. If we don't get him in there tonight we're sunk!'

'I been wondering how to tell him anyway.'

'Me too. I suppose the twins might know where he is . . .'

The Peretti twins, Angela and Zerlina, were a year or two younger than the others. They had attached themselves to the New Cut Gang some time ago, and for all Benny's scorn of kids (apart from Sharky Bob) he had a healthy respect for their sharp wits, not to mention their ferocity. You wouldn't think they were fierce to look at them; they looked like little Italian angels, with big innocent brown eyes and masses of black curly hair; but when they were roused, they were worse than African Sam, whose temper was legendary.

And more to the point, Dippy was fond of them. They might be able to persuade him even if the boys couldn't.

'Yeah,' said Thunderbolt. 'Good idea.'

The two boys set off like greyhounds. They found the twins arguing with Snake-Eyes Melmott the bookie outside the Welsh Harp, dragged them away, and told them the whole story in fifty seconds flat.

'Right!' said Angela. 'We'll find him.'

'We'll make him do it if it's the last thing he does,' said Zerlina.

They raced up and down the New Cut, and along

Lower Marsh, and saw a hot-pea man and a muffin-man and a pie-man, but no Dippy. Then they charged up one side of Waterloo Road as far as the railway bridge and down the other as far as St George's Circus, and then back up again, and finally they ran into him coming out of Chippin's the greengrocer's on the corner of Webber Row.

'Dippy! Listen—'

'Dippy, you got to do summing for us—'

'You gotta be a public benefactor!'

'It's heroic, Dippy, and only you can do it!'

Dippy blinked at them suspiciously.

'Wot?' he said.

'It's easy, honest,' said Thunderbolt, tugging his sleeve.

'I'll push yer stove for yer, Dippy,' said Benny.

Dippy feebly allowed the twins to lead him along the crowded pavement behind his hot stove.

'But . . .' he said.

'There's nothing to it, Dip,' said Angela. 'It's not as if we're asking you to shin up a drainpipe or crawl through a sewer—'

'Or get shot at or stabbed——' said Zerlina.

'Or hanged, or poisoned,' said Benny. 'Or suffer the Death of a Thousand Cuts, like that bloke in the Waxworks.'

They didn't stop talking until they reached Clayton Terrace. They parked Dippy's stove in the backyard and went into Thunderbolt's kitchen, where Bridie was waiting by the light of a candle with scissors and flour and rouge and a jar of dripping.

'Woss this all about then?' said Dippy, profoundly suspicious. 'Woss that dripping for?'

'Yer hair, of course!' said Bridie. 'It won't lie flat on its own, and we can't afford proper macassar oil. Now sit down and——'

He goggled.

'Me *hair*?'

'And the flour's for yer cheeks — no! Don't let him run away! Sit down, Dippy. Do as ye're told!'

Since she had a pair of scissors in her hand, and since she was her mother's daughter, he sat down at once. The twins held him down while she worked on him. Benny, meanwhile, was taking a suit out of a bag. He'd

borrowed it from his father's workshop, since the customer it was being altered for had to go away rather suddenly for his health, so he obviously didn't want it. Benny shook it out with practised hands, swung it this way and that to admire the nap of the cloth, and brushed a fleck or two of dust from the black shoulders.

While he was doing that, Thunderbolt polished his father's best pair of boots. Mr Dobney had great big feet, so Dippy was bound to be comfortable in them.

'You're going to look like the Duke of Clarence,' said Benny admiringly.

'I hope not,' said Dippy. 'He's dead.'

'Well, before he was dead. Nice schmutter, this. Look at the cut, eh!'

'I wish I knew what you was doing,' Dippy mumbled.

Thunderbolt stopped polishing to gaze at the change Bridie was working on Dippy's face. His moustache – a great ragged thing like the back end of a dirty dog – was trim and tidy; his grimy all-weather complexion had been whitened to the colour of plaster-of-Paris with the flour and then given a healthy pink glow with the rouge, and his straggly grey hair was pasted flat with the dripping.

'H'mm,' said Bridie, her head on one side.

'He looks . . . distinguished,' said Angela.

'He looks embalmed,' said Zerlina.

'I know what it is!' said Bridie suddenly. 'It's his barnet.'

'Not more dripping?' said Dippy helplessly.

But Sharky Bob was scraping out the dripping pot: there was none left. Anyway, that wasn't what Bridie had in mind.

'It's too grey,' she said. 'Ye look shockin' old with grey hair.'

'I *am* shockin' old!'

'Yeah, but that won't do tonight. Ye gotta look young and fit and healthy. Give us that boot-polish, Thunderbolt . . .'

'But why? Why?' Dippy gave a groan and closed his eyes.

Taking no notice, she opened the tin of blacking. With the help of a table-knife she spread the sticky black substance on Dippy's hair, smoothing it artistically and running the back of the knife-blade along the parting.

When that was done, they made him stand up and got the suit on his nerveless limbs, and then made him step into Mr Dobney's boots. Then Angela adjusted the celluloid collar and Zerlina tied the tasteful lime-green and violet cravat.

They all gazed in awe. A shiny, porcelain-like glaze covered Dippy's features; the boot-polish and the dripping had combined into a glistening, varnished, jet-black sheet over the top of his head.

'Miraculous,' said Benny. 'You're a star, Dippy.' Three or four money-making schemes darted like hummingbirds through the tropical jungle of Benny's brain, but he ignored them; there'd be plenty more. 'Listen, we couldn't have picked a better night for it. That Mr Paget's been rearranging the windows. They'll never notice!'

The old man's eyes rolled from one to the other of them. His cheeks were too stiffly pasted for him to speak easily, but a flicker of alarm showed in his bloodshot eyes.

'Winders?' he said. 'What winders?'

'Oh, yeah,' said Benny. 'We better tell you the rest of the plan. Sit down, Dip, old boy. Thunderbolt, guard the door . . .'

'Oh no! No! Absolutely not!'

'Oh yes! You *got* to!'

'I refuse!'

'You can't, you promised!'

'I never promised—'

'He did, didn't he? Didn't he promise?'

'Dippy, this is a matter of public honour!'

'It's a matter of shame and humiliation, you mean! Me stand in Rummage's window? Like a ruddy mannequin? Oh, no. Oh, no. Never in a thousand years. You must be stark raving . . . Well, you *are*, I know you are, all of yer, imps of Satan, tormentin' me! Get thee behind me! Help!'

'Dippy,' said Bridie sternly, 'if ye don't do as ye're told I swear I'll think up a hideous vengeance.'

'Cut his livers out,' suggested Angela.

'He's only got one,' said Zerlina. 'You're thinking of kidneys.'

'Them and all. Cut 'em out and hang 'em on his hot-chestnut stove. That'd teach him a lesson.'

Dippy groaned and tottered.

'I don't believe what's happenin',' he muttered. 'This must be an evil vision brought on by drink. I'll never touch it again, I swear . . .'

'No, it ain't, Dippy, and you're no drunkard,' said Bridie urgently. 'It's real. So listen, you old clot. You got a job to do.'

Dippy's eyes swivelled pleadingly from one to another of them and found no mercy. Even Sharky Bob was feeling the edge of his spoon as if it was a dagger, and frowning like a buccaneer.

'Oh, all right,' Dippy muttered. 'I know when I'm beat.'

They all sat down. Thunderbolt stayed near the door in case Dippy made a run for it, and Benny looked at the old tin clock on the mantelpiece.

'What's the time? Six o'clock? That's good. We got two hours before Rummage's closes. Now listen,

Dippy. You know these snide coins? Well, a feller called Stamper Billings made 'em sixteen years ago and hid 'em in the basement where Rummage's is now. And Rummage found 'em and he passes 'em out in the change, and no one knows except us, and we're gonna catch him. So we made him think he oughter make the coins look old else he'll be found out, and he's gonna do it tonight . . . And we got a secret weapon. Look!'

And he produced, with a flourish, the detective camera that belonged to Messrs Grover and Cohen, and which had taken him half an hour's solid pestering to borrow. It was flat circular object bound in dark leather. You wore it hanging on your chest with the lens poking out through a buttonhole on your waistcoat, and you exposed each picture by pulling a ring at the bottom.

'Now listen, Dippy,' he went on, 'we gotta get in and photograph Rummage with those coins, but we can't hide in the shop and wait 'cause he won't let us in in the first place. So we need someone in there first to unbolt the door and let us in. So—'

'Catch him!' said Bridie, and the twins each seized a leg as Dippy made for the window.

There was a brief struggle, in the course of which the candle was knocked over. It went out at once.

'Got him?' said Benny. 'Sit him down, then. Thunderbolt, where's the matches?'

'I only got one match left.'

'We'll just have to sit in the dark, then,' said Benny. 'Dippy? You listening?'

An inarticulate moan made its way out of Dippy's lips.

'Good. 'Cause it's gotta be *you* what hides in there and—'

'Sssh!'

It was Bridie, and she laid a strong hand on Benny's arm to emphasize the message.

'What's that noise outside?' she whispered.

Everyone fell still. In the yard outside the kitchen window someone was whispering, and then there came the unmistakable sound of fingernails on the window-frame, feeling for the way in.

Then there was a cracking, splintered sound followed by a whispered, 'You sure this is the right house?'

The other man whispered back, 'Yeah. It's right under that noisy old trot Mary Malone.'

Thunderbolt heard a soft intake of breath from Bridie. Benny made a signal, and all the kids sank to hide in a crouch behind the table and the rocking-chair. In the dim light through the oilcloth blind Thunderbolt could see Dippy, still sitting in his chair in a trance of fear, like a rabbit mesmerized by a snake.

'And you're sure they brung it here?' said the first voice.

'I seen 'em! The kid with the glasses had it under his arm . . .'

They're talking about the dummy! Thunderbolt thought in astonishment, and from the wide eyes gleaming beside him, he saw that the others were equally surprised. And then there was a soft tinkling sound as the glass fell to the floor, and the oilcloth blind was raised cautiously.

Crouching very still, the kids saw two heads outlined against the sky. Then one man struck a match and lit a bull's-eye lantern. The smell of hot oil drifted into the room, and then a ray of light shone out full on the still figure of Dippy.

'That's it!' came a hoarse whisper.

'You sure?'

'Yeah! Horrible ugly thing. I'd know it anywhere. Get in quick and stuff it in the—'

But Thunderbolt could hold back no longer. Invading his home! Planning to steal his property! Normally he was sure he was the most timid person in the whole of Lambeth, but out of somewhere a great rage burst up in him, and he yelled with fury and leaped at the burglar.

And then there was confusion. Finding the darkness inhabited by several imps or demons with whirling fists and savage teeth (Sharky having connected with a leg) instead of a placid wax dummy, the invaders shouted in horrible terror and scrambled towards the open window. A hideous clatter of pots and pans – devilish yells and roars – the rip of the oilcloth tearing from top to bottom – the crash of the upturned table; and then both men were in the yard, bleating with fear, and leaping over the wall and making off down the alley.

Windows were flung open all around, and faces peered down curiously.

'Bridie!' came a mighty roar from above, and the kids, picking themselves up off the damp stones of the yard or leaning out of the kitchen window, saw the huge form of Mrs Malone looking down, surrounded by clouds of steamy light. 'What the divil's going on?'

'Burglars, Ma,' Bridie called up cheerfully. 'We chased 'em off.'

'I'm glad to hear it. Where's the boy?'

'Hello!' shouted Sharky Bob. 'I et a leg, Ma!'

'Let's hope it wasn't poisoned,' said Mrs Malone, and banged the window shut.

The kids clambered back to find Dippy rigid with fear. He slowly opened one eye.

'They gorn?' he whispered.

'That's the third time someone's been after that dummy,' said Bridie.

'There's more to this than meets the eye,' said Angela.

'Never mind that now,' said Benny impatiently. 'We better get Dippy over to Rummage's and settled in that window.'

Thunderbolt looked around the kitchen and twisted

his lips at the damage. A broken window, a torn blind, and the big saucepan had a dent that wasn't there before; but there was something more worrying than that.

'Listen,' he said to no one in particular, 'those blokes must've been tipped off.'

'Probably more art collectors,' said Benny impatiently. 'Probably going to put it in a private museum. But never mind that now. Come on, else Rummage's'll be closing.'

'No! *Listen!*' said Thunderbolt. 'What do they want the dummy *for*? I reckon they're gonna try the same trick! I reckon they know we're on Rummage's trail!'

'I bet they don't,' said Bridie. 'No one knows that.'

'Come *on!*' said Benny, fizzing with impatience.

He tugged Dippy's arm. The twins followed, but Thunderbolt hung back; he was still puzzled about this interest in the dummy.

And so was Bridie.

'That French geezer, that monsewer in the stable,' she said, 'he didn't look like a burgular. I don't think he's connected with this last lot at all. And the first bloke that took it – I'll swear that was Sid the Swede. These blokes were different.'

'It's a mystery,' said Thunderbolt. 'I reckon it's as much of a mystery as—'

'Oh! I nearly forgot!' she said, fishing a little metal flask out of her pocket. 'Take this, and give Dippy a drop if he comes over faint. It's Uncle Paddy's horse-reviver. He gave it to old Charlie Maggott's mare when she wouldn't run.'

'But aren't you coming?'

'I just want to have another look at the dummy. I'll come on after.'

Before he left, Thunderbolt reached up to his Museum and took out his lump of criminal lead. He hardly knew why he was doing it: he had the vague idea that he could drop it in the gutter and pretend it had nothing to do with him.

'Come *on*, Thunderbolt!' said Angela, coming back to drag at his arm.

'Yeah, I'm coming . . .'

They caught up with the others at the end of Herriot Street, just around the corner from Rummage's. Dippy had a bowler hat pulled down so low, and a muffler pulled up so high, that all you could see between them were two watery eyes and a pointy, white, glistening nose that looked as if it would break off if it knocked against anything. He was shuffling along in Mr Dobney's boots, unable to lift his feet because he left the boots behind when he did.

'You must have really little feet, Dippy,' said Angela. 'Like a chest of drawers or summing.'

'Never mind his trotter-boxes,' said Benny. 'Once he gets in that window he can take 'em off if he wants to. I wouldn't be surprised if Rummage's gonna close a bit earlier tonight. I bet he's anxious. I bet he's consumed by guilt. I bet he feels shockin' nervous.'

Dippy had begun to tremble. Thunderbolt saw his knees shaking in the tight trousers, and then he heard a clicking sound, which was Dippy's four teeth going.

'What's he doing? He's not *shivering?* You can't have a shivering dummy, it'd give the game away at once!' said Benny, disconcerted.

'He better have some of this,' said Thunderbolt.

'Eh? Wossat?' said Dippy.

'It's Bridie's Uncle Paddy's horse-reviver,' explained Thunderbolt. 'I should think one good swig'd set you up for an hour, at least.'

Dippy inserted the flask between the muffler and the hat-brim. There was a brief sucking noise and then a gasp.

'Nice, Dippy?' said Zerlina.

He couldn't speak. 'Ah – ah—' he murmured faintly, and handed back the flask. Benny took a sniff at it and made a face. But whatever it had done for Charlie Maggott's mare, the horse-reviver had certainly fortified Dippy. He shuffled bravely forward, head held high in order to see under the hat-brim.

They stopped by the bright gaslit windows of the big store, where crowds of customers struggled to get through the crowds coming out. Thunderbolt felt a rush of anger: here was Mr Rummage, making all the money he must be making, and still he was so mean that he couldn't resist passing out snide coins and having another man punished for it.

'Do yer best, Dippy!' he said.

'You got that horse-reviver?' Dippy muttered.

'Give him the flask,' said Angela.

Thunderbolt passed it over.

'D'you think that's a good idea?' said Zerlina.

'It's only a little flask,' said Benny. 'It's good for him, I expect. It smells horrible so it's bound to be.'

They saw the sense of that, all having experienced medicines of uncommon vileness in their time.

'Good luck, Dippy!' said Thunderbolt.

And Dippy put the flask in his pocket and shuffled forward into the great shop. No King or Queen had ever felt more proud of their army on the way to battle than the New Cut Gang felt of Dippy Hitchcock then, as he weaved uncertainly through the crowds and into the very jaws of danger.

Five

Hiccups, Wasps and Straw

Dippy Hitchcock had led a peaceful, unambitious life up till then. The most dangerous thing that had ever happened to him was nearly getting knocked over by a sheep. That had been early one morning, when he was visiting his cousin Ted in Newbury, and a flock of sheep being driven to market had come up the road at a fast gallop. A particularly savage old ewe had made for Dippy as if intending to trample him to death, and he'd skipped out of the way just in time. Apart from that he'd led a placid life.

So going into Rummage's on a daring mission like this was making his poor old heart skip about like a grasshopper. The further in he went, the more he felt the need for another nip of horse-reviver. Perhaps when he was in the window . . .

But getting in the window wasn't going to be easy. It looked simple enough from outside – there was a little door at the back of the window-space that obviously led into the shop; but what you couldn't see from the street was that the little doors opened behind the counters. He'd have to get behind a counter first, and there was a swarm of shop-assistants already there, who'd be bound to think it odd if a strange wax-like figure clambered over to join them. It wasn't the sort of thing you'd miss.

Then there was the problem of which window to pick. There were six of them, and to the best of Dippy's recollection, only one of them showed men's clothing. Of the others, one displayed china dinner services, another bicycles, another bamboo furniture, and the last two displayed ladies' wear. The thought of finding himself in the window with the ladies' nightclothes made Dippy break out into a cold sweat. This was very unfortunate, because the sweat combined with the flour on his face to make a sort of gluey porridge which slowly seeped downwards, making him look as if he was melting. People who saw him shuddered and said, 'Poor man.'

So which window should it be? The most likely one was the one whose little door opened behind the Gentlemen's Outfitting. However, presiding over the other side of the counter was the man Benny and the gang had seen arranging the window on the evening they got the first coin: Mr Paget the Gentlemen's Outfitting Manager. He'd fixed a suspicious eye on Dippy the second the old man had come into view. In his experience, people with that many clothes on only intended to hide things in them, and if ever he'd seen a shoplifter, it was this shady-looking individual in the big boots.

Then Mr Paget blinked, peered more closely, and found his suspicions confirmed. The wretch was wearing a mask!

The staff at Rummage's were always being urged to look out for shoplifters, and Mr Rummage even offered a Thieftaker's Bonus to any assistant who caught one in the act. Mr Paget felt every nerve in his body twitch with the prospect of earning the Thieftaker's Bonus. He snapped his fingers to summon his assistant from the other end of the counter, where he'd been putting away some gloves.

'Leave them gloves and take charge of the counter, Wilkins,' he said. 'I shall only be a few minutes.'

He lifted the wooden flap and stepped through, moving, as he thought, with the caution of a jungle cat. His eyes never left Dippy for a moment. He began to track the old man from department to department, as Dippy blundered blearily from the Gentlemen's Outfitting to the Haberdashery to the Soft Furnishings, and back again, occasionally bouncing gently off the nearest fitting, and every so often stopping to refresh himself with the horse-reviver. Mr Paget, eyes gleaming, moustache bristling, teeth bared like a tiger's, followed him at a short distance, moving in a silent prowl and darting for concealment from place to place.

This might have gone on until the shop closed, but two things happened. Firstly a customer loudly demanded to see some gloves, so Mr Paget's assistant had to leave that part of the counter and attend to him at the other end.

Secondly, another customer tapped Mr Paget on the shoulder when he was being particularly tiger-like behind a delicately balanced display of glassware.

Mr Paget leaped like a dog discovered eating from the cat's bowl. His arm nudged the top shelf of the glassware display, and a cascade of crystal decanters, salt-cellars, goblets and tumblers fell to the floor with a mighty crash. Mr Paget gave a yelp of dismay, and tried simultaneously to pick up the broken glass, answer the customer's question, and keep an eye on Dippy; but he couldn't do all three, and Dippy was gone.

By now, Dippy had applied so much of the horse-reviver that he was more or less oblivious to falling glassware. Finding himself in the Gentlemen's Outfitting yet again, and seeing the counter unmanned, he vaguely remembered that he had something to do through that little door on the other side.

He clambered over the counter, fell heavily behind it, got up cheerfully, opened the wooden door and was through in a moment.

He found himself in a curious narrow space lit by hissing gaslights, occupied by four or five men standing or sitting very stiffly and wearing smart clothes. There was a big glass wall a couple of feet away, through which he could dimly see crowds of people passing to and fro, and that and the other men in there put him in mind of something.

'Here,' he said to the man standing closest, 'is this the Waxworks?'

The man didn't speak.

'Oi,' said Dippy, and prodded him.

The man fell over.

Dippy thought he'd killed him. He was horrified.

'Sorry!' he gasped. 'I didn't mean to kill yer! Here – have a nip of horse-reviver . . .'

He struggled past the man seated nearby and offered the flask to the dead man. Suddenly a suspicion struck him.

'Here,' he said, 'you're a wossname, ain't yer!'

He flicked the man's nose. A hollow knocking sound came from it.

'Ahh,' said Dippy. 'Thassit. I member now. I'm a dummy. Well, you stay there, mate, out the way, and I'll take yer plate. Tape yer place. That.'

He stood up cautiously. No one seemed to have noticed. The other men in the little space were obviously pretending to be dummies as well.

'Not a word, eh?' said Dippy to the nearest one, and winked. 'Prime lark, this is. Gissa bit o' room . . .'

He nudged the man slightly, and he fell over too. Dippy shook his head sadly.

'Drunk,' he said to himself. 'Shockin'.'

He had another nip of the horse-reviver. There didn't seem to be much left. Still, the chair was vacant now, and he could sit down.

He was vaguely aware that there were people watching – that in fact a small crowd was gathering outside the glass. Normally he'd have felt shy, but being a waxwork (he'd forgotten the shop-window plan, and his mind had wandered back to the Waxworks) he didn't feel shy at all. In fact, he thought, I've got quite a talent for this business.

He arranged himself comfortably, legs elegantly crossed, hands on hips, and gazed out at the crowd. He couldn't see them very well. All he could really see was a reflection of himself, and very fine I look too, he thought. He raised his head a little, tilted his chin to one side, loosened the fit of the jacket over his shoulders, and settled into a trance-like stillness.

Outside, PC Jellicoe the local constable was urging the crowd to move on.

'Make way there! Come on, move along! Clear the way! Clear the way!'

They protested, but PC Jellicoe took no notice. Lot of nonsense! Perfectly ordinary shop-window display. Rather stylish, if anything, but not worth gathering a crowd for.

'Move along! Move along!'

The crowd dispersed reluctantly.

Benny, Thunderbolt and the twins, watching from across the street, sighed with relief as the crowd moved away.

'He's done it!' said Benny. 'That's the first problem out of the way.'

'He's gotta stay there for a long time yet,' said Zerlina doubtfully. 'And people keep looking at him . . . Are they going to leave the window lights on all night?'

'Dunno. What's that little boy staring at?'

For a small boy was tugging at his mother's hand just outside Dippy's window.

'Mummy! Mummy! Look at that dummy! It's got hiccups!' he said in a piercing voice that reached across the street.

'Oh Septimus, *really* . . .' said the mother, stopping reluctantly.

Benny and Thunderbolt listened apprehensively and

sidled across the street to see what was going on. Two urchins, who'd seen the nauseating Septimus in his sailor-suit and had come up intent on mayhem, were staring at Dippy instead.

'Cor! Look at him!'

'Must be a mechanical one . . .'

Dippy, legs crossed elegantly, eyes happily vacant, was sitting perfectly still; except that every ten seconds or so his body jerked as if an electric current had been applied to the chair. Soon the urchins, and the sailor-suited Septimus, were counting and joining in.

'Nine – ten – HIC!'

'That was a good 'un! He'll fall over in a minute!'

'Eight – nine – HIC!'

'I heard that one through the glass!'

'How'd they do it?'

'I reckon compressed air.'

'HIC!'

'Or hydraulics. Betcher there's a tube going up his trolleywags—'

'HIC!'

'Septimus, come *on*! This is not the way to behave!'

'Mummy, what are trolleywags?'

'That's *enough*!'

Benny and Thunderbolt exchanged an uneasy glance. Further down the street, PC Jellicoe had seen the crowd beginning to form again, and was strolling majestically back to disperse it for the second time.

Since that was the last thing they wanted, Benny took the initiative by whipping the caps off the two urchins' heads and running across the street.

'Oi!'

'Oo done that?'

'There he goes—'

'Get 'im!'

Hiccups forgotten, the urchins gave chase. Benny led them along the New Cut and left into Waterloo Road, where he chucked the caps into the back of a dustcart that happened to be passing. There was a brisk exchange of threats and insults, and the urchins raced off after their caps; so that was one problem dealt with.

There were plenty more to come.

Mr Paget was dealing with a problem at that very moment inside the shop. In his excitement after knocking over the glassware and losing Dippy, he rushed about challenging everyone who looked remotely like him. He'd challenged three men in black overcoats and insisted on prodding the face of one of them because he said it looked like a mask; and the

customer had made such a fuss that Mr Rummage himself had to come and sort it out.

'I have never been so insulted!' the customer was
bellowing.

'I am truly sorry,' Mr Paget kept saying, squirming
and bowing and trying to escape by walking backwards.
'I deeply and humbly beg your pardon, but the fact is
that your face does look as if—'

'*What?* How dare you? How dare you, sir?' the
customer demanded.

Mr Paget squirmed and cringed even more, and
backed into a dummy advertising 'Dux-Bak' rainwear,
sending it crashing to the floor.

Mr Rummage merely looked at him and raised his
eyebrows. When he did that he looked terrifying.

'Well?' he said.

'Yes! I'll pick it up! Sorry! Sorry!'

Mr Paget gathered the 'Dux-Bak' dummy in his
arms and laid it on the counter like corpse in a funeral
parlour.

'I'll mend it!' he babbled, sweating at the thought
of all the damage he'd done. 'I'll stay behind and

mend it personally myself on my own without any help!'

'You've done quite enough damage already,' said Mr Rummage, who had his own reasons for not wanting anyone on the premises after closing time. 'Go! Go on! Leave!'

Mortified, Mr Paget slunk away and left.

By now it was time to close. Mr Rummage ushered out the rest of the staff and went over the whole shop, locking doors and windows, peering suspiciously into cupboards, cloakrooms, lifts, into every corner that might have concealed an intruder or a policeman.

Finally he went to check the main doors again, and had a nasty shock, because peering through the glass at him were four pairs of eyes.

He nearly dropped the lantern he was carrying, but caught it in time and hurried to the door to chase the eyes away. They seemed to belong to a pack of children. They scattered in all directions as he opened the door, but then Mr Rummage heard a burst of laughter from the left, and looked along the front of the shop to see a group of idle good-for-nothing rascals hooting with laughter outside one of his windows.

How dare they! He gaped in amazement as they slapped their thighs, held their sides, bent double with merriment, pointing and making strange slapping movements with their hands.

'Constable! Constable!' he shouted, and set off at once to see what was the matter.

PC Jellicoe, who was built more for solidity than for speed, was getting fed up. This was the third time he'd had to come and sort out these customers of Mr Rummage's, and he had the rest of his beat to see to. He lumbered back and looked down at Mr Rummage disapprovingly.

'If you can't control your customers, Mr Rummage,' he said, 'I shall have to ask you to cover your windows up.'

'They're not my customers! I don't allow riff-raff like that into my emporium! While they're in the street they're the responsibility of the law, and I want them moved on, d'you hear?'

PC Jellicoe sniffed majestically, but since he

couldn't think of anything to say in reply, he merely nodded austerely and sauntered along to the little crowd around the window.

From across the street, Benny and Thunderbolt and the twins, lurking in the shadows of Targett's Alley, watched in despair.

'Oi! Move along!' PC Jellicoe was saying. 'Clear the way there! You'll be facing a charge of obstruction if you don't move along!'

'But Constable, look at him!'

'It's as good as a play—'

'Move along!'

'But he's—'

'He's done it again! There he goes!'

'Cor, he nearly got it that time . . .'

All the spectators, in between their chortling, were swinging their arms about and slapping at the air. The constable raised his voice.

'This has the making of a scene of civil disobedience of the most reprehensible type. Be about your lawful business, else I shall be compelled to read the Riot Act and start making arrests.'

He was longing to look in the window and see what they were laughing at, but he feared that he might want to join in, which would be beneath his dignity.

If he had, he'd have seen Dippy still sitting on his chair, cured of his hiccups now but troubled by a wasp which had been slumbering in a dusty corner for months and had just woken up. It had taken a fancy to the pink of Dippy's cheeks, and kept trying to land there and see what they tasted like; and Dippy kept hearing it approach and swatting violently at the air, nearly losing his balance, and then trying to be still again.

When the onlookers had moved away, laughing and going *bzzz* at each other and slapping the air, PC Jellicoe finally turned to look in the window. By chance that coincided with a moment when the wasp was having a rest on the nose of one of the other dummies, and there was nothing moving but Dippy's eyes, swivelling wildly in their sockets because the wasp was just out of his line of sight and he had the uneasy feeling that it was walking down his neck.

PC Jellicoe saw Dippy's eyes move, and blinked and rubbed his own. But when he looked again the eyes were looking straight ahead – staring directly at him, in fact – and so unsettling was the effect of Dippy's disintegrating flour-caked cheeks and goggling bloodshot eyes that the constable took a step backwards in shock.

He hoped no one had seen him. He had half a mind to go and tell Mr Rummage to take the horrible thing out of the window as a danger to traffic. It was probably some new fashion, but if a nervous horse caught sight of it, it could easily cause an accident.

However, Mr Rummage had gone back into the

shop, and the doors were locked. PC Jellicoe tested them all in order to look efficient, settled his helmet more firmly on his perspiring head, and strode off towards the Blackfriars Road at the regulation three miles an hour, leaving the road clear.

'Thank goodness for that!' breathed Benny. 'But what's that old clot Dippy up to?'

'I think he's signalling to us in semaphore,' said Thunderbolt. 'He's done X, and T, and Z, and F so far.'

'Well he can't spell then,' said Benny. 'I wish Rummage'd turn the bloomin' lights off. Then Dippy could slip out and open the doors. And where's Bridie? Seems to me you can't rely on anyone!'

As a matter of fact, Bridie was extremely busy. She and Sharky Bob were investigating the other mystery: that of the waxwork model that two lots of crooks, three if you counted the Frenchman, were after.

'What I reckon, Sharky,' she said, 'is that someone's got hold of this while Thunderbolt's back was turned, and hidden something in it.'

'Maybe dimonds,' he said.

'Yeah, could be. 'Cause it certainly ain't worth nothing on its own. So we oughter open it up, seems to me, and have a look.'

They were upstairs, having lugged the dummy up there for safety. The rest of the family were all crowded into the kitchen, where Uncle Paddy had the whistle going and Mr Sweeny was playing the fiddle, so for the moment the bedroom Bridie shared with five others was empty.

She set the candle-stump on the chest of drawers and hauled the dummy on the bed. It had got pretty battered in all its adventures, and it hadn't been beautiful to begin with, she had to admit.

'Take his clothes off,' said Sharky.

'Yeah, I'm going to. What's that ye're eating?'

'His ear,' said Sharky. 'It come off in me hand.'

'Well, what was yer hand doing on his ear in the first place?'

'Pulling it off,' he said. There was a grand simplicity about Sharky Bob.

'Oh, for goodness' sake ... Eat it then. I don't suppose it'll do ye any harm, the amount of terrible rubbish ye've packed down yer manhole already. Now move back out the way. I'm going to try and get his clothes off without making them look any shabbier . . .'

Happily munching on the wax ear, Sharky sat on Siobhan's side of the mattress and watched Bridie wrestling with the dummy's clothes. She got them off eventually, and felt in the pockets, but the only thing there was a paper bag that had once contained boiled sweets. She gave it to Sharky to smell.

Then she felt along the coarse sacking sausage-shapes that were the dummy's arms and legs. In one leg she found a half-eaten turnip, and in the other she found a length of twine with an immense and complicated knot in it. She recognized it as the one Thunderbolt had used when he'd thought of taking up escapology. They'd spent forty minutes tying him up, and he'd taken three and a half hours to get loose; which, as Benny said, was a bit long to expect a music-hall audience to watch a kind of lump heaving and grunting. Thunderbolt had tired of escapology, and thrown the twine away, and here it was again. But not even Benny would imagine that gangs of crazed knot-fanciers would take desperate measures to steal it.

She threw the knotted twine into the corner and continued the surgery.

'Try his belly,' said Sharky Bob. 'I bet there's dimonds in his belly. That's where I'd put 'em, in the belly.'

'That's where you put everything, Sharky.'

'Yeah,' he said.

But the belly held only straw, and so did the chest and the arms. By the time she'd got to the neck, the bedroom was covered in wisps of hay and cornstalks and ragged bunches of straw and bits of sacking. The head on its broomstick spine stared up reproachfully through its one remaining blood-alley eye.

Bridie scratched her own head and stared back at it.

Then she plucked off the ear that Sharky hadn't eaten and twisted it this way and that. It was funny stuff; sort of sooty streaks in it; soft but not sticky; and it did have a smell, or was she imagining it?

She sniffed at it. It did have a smell, and quite a strong one, too, but it was nice. In fact it was very nice. No wonder all those dogs had been so keen to get at it. The more she rubbed it between her fingers and thumb, the stronger and the nicer it smelled.

'I wonder . . .' she said.

'It can't . . .' she went on.

'I don't suppose . . .' she muttered.

Then a light seemed to switch itself on in her head. She slapped the ear back in place and clapped her hands.

'Come on, Sharky!' she cried. 'I got it! I know what they were after!'

And she thrust the head, horsehair whiskers and blood-alley eye and all, into an old cotton shopping bag and swept Sharky off the bed and down the stairs.

Six

'It Screamed at Me!'

By this time, the kids in the alley opposite Rummage's were hopping with impatience. Dippy couldn't creep out while people were looking, and the window seemed to act as a magnet for all kinds of passers-by.

Including dogs. A suspicious-natured cur called Rags, who belonged to Fred Hipkiss the grocer, caught sight of Dippy's face as he stopped to investigate a lamppost. Rags suddenly leaped backwards, all his mangy hair stood on end, and a low growl came from his throat as he stalked up to the window. After his trouble with the hiccups and the wasp, Dippy was feeling rather sleepy, and gave a sudden jerk as he nearly nodded off. That roused Rags's fury. Clearly the horrible thing in there was challenging him to a fight. He leaped up at the window time and time again, barking madly, tumbling down each time only to get up in a frenzy of noise and temper and try again. Benny dealt with that; he ran across, lassoed Rags with Thunderbolt's emergency twine, and hauled him away.

The next problem was a young man called Ernest and his best girl, Ethel. They were strolling along moonily, stopping every so often to look at each other and sigh. Finally they drifted to a halt outside Dippy's window and gazed into each other's eyes. The kids tiptoed across and hid in the angle of the bow window near by.

'Oh, Ernest,' Ethel sighed.

'Oh, Ethel,' Ernest mumbled.

'D'you love me, Ernest?'

'Oh, yes!'

'How much do you love me?'

'Oh . . . A *yuge* amount. Enormous.'

'Would you save me from a burning building?'

'Not half!'

'What else would you do for me, Ernest?'

'I'd . . .' Ernest paused.

'What?'

'Ethel, you see that dummy in the window?'

The gang froze. Ethel drew back her head from Ernest's shoulder.

'What about it?' she said.

'Well them gloves it's got on, they're just like the ones I told you about what I saw in Whiteley's.'

'Is that *all*? You're more interested in gloves than in me! I don't know why I bother with you – you don't love me at all!'

'I do! I do! Honest!'

'Well, what would you do for me?'

'I'd . . . I'd . . . Ethel, I'd swim the fiercest river in the world!'

'What else?'

'I'd . . . I'd run a thousand miles in me bare feet!'

'And?'

'I'd fight ten lions with me bare hands!'

'Oh, Ernest!' Ethel said softly. 'And when can I see you again?'

'Well, I'll come on Tuesday if it isn't raining,' he said.

'*Ohhhh!*'

And Ethel stamped her foot and flounced away. Ernest followed, protesting.

'Helpless!' said Angela. 'Run a thousand miles, fight ten lions . . .'

'And he'll come on Tuesday if it isn't raining. Huh!' Zerlina scoffed.

'Never mind them,' said Benny. 'What we gonna do about Dippy?'

'He's paralysed!' said Thunderbolt. 'It's that horse-reviver – it must've turned his blood to ice!'

'He's not moving at all!' said Benny. 'Wake up, you old clot!'

Dippy awoke with a loud snort. He blinked and looked around, and Benny tapped the glass again. Dippy peered forward and finally saw a row of desperate faces through the window. They were all saying something that he couldn't make out. Get to the floor? Give to the poor?

Then they started gesturing at him. He thought

they'd gone mad. He was about to say so to the man sitting next to him, when he had a horrible shock: *the man was dead!* Some horrible murder had been committed – a deranged taxidermist had stuffed the victim and sat him up in a chair – and he'd be next—

With a help of terror, Dippy tried to escape. He uncrossed his legs and stood up ... But having been crossed for so long, the left one had gone to sleep, and when Dippy put his weight on it, it gave way.

'They've cut me leg off!' he gasped, grabbing at the nearest thing, which happened to be one of the other two dummies left standing. It fell over with him, and the two of them landed locked in an embrace which made Dippy think of 'The Mummy's Vengeance', a story he'd read only the month before in one of Thunderbolt's penny shockers.

Incoherent with terror, he scrambled up, found the little door, wrenched it open, and tumbled through into the darkness of the shop, giving out little squeaks of fear.

The darkness was cool and quiet. Dippy still

couldn't stand up straight, because his leg hadn't woken up. Maybe if he had just a little sip of the horse-reviver ... There was still a bit left in the flask.

He swallowed the last mouthful, smacking his lips with satisfaction.

Someone behind him was shouting. Wasn't it Benny's voice?

'Swallow some more!'

Or was it: 'Open the door?'

Yes! That was it! He had to open the door. Nothing to it, really ... He laughed a scornful laugh, thinking of how fearful he'd been.

Just get over the counter, and he could open the door and go home and have a lie-down, same as that other fellow was doing further along.

That other fellow was the 'Dux-Bak' Rainwear dummy which Mr Paget had put there earlier, but to Dippy's fuddled eyes it looked so comfortable lying there that he thought he'd join it. At the third try he got on to the polished mahogany counter, knocking off a display rack of 'Silk-O-Lene' cravats on the way, and stretched himself out peacefully. He fell asleep at once.

* * *

Meanwhile, alone in the basement, Mr Rummage was feverishly shovelling sixpences and shillings and half-crowns out of a tea-chest and into a Gladstone bag. Ever since he'd discovered the stash, hidden away under a trapdoor in the Ironmongery Department, he'd been torn between gloating over his good luck and trembling in case he was found out. And when he'd heard those two plain-clothes detectives this morning dropping hints that they were on to him, he'd been itching to get down here and dispose of the loot. If he could get the coins home to his comfortable house in Streatham, he could hide them there safely till the danger had passed.

He scooped up the last few sixpences with a 'Skoopitup' enamelled dustpan, shut the Gladstone bag with a snap and replaced the trapdoor. Then he hauled a heavy 'Skweezitout' mangle over to stand on top of it, looked around critically to make sure that he hadn't left any sixpences on the floor, and turned off the one hissing gaslight.

Nearly done, he thought. Soon to be safe. He picked

up the Gladstone bag, tiptoed to the stairs – and then froze.

Burglars!

There were noises from the floor above – muffled thuds and mutterings of a sort which wouldn't have been made by any honest person. Mr Rummage bit his lip. He wasn't afraid of burglars, but if he had to call a policeman while carrying a Gladstone bag full of snide coins ...

Perhaps he could scare them away without involving the police.

Pausing only to take a 'Slysitoff' silver-plated carving knife from a nearby rack of kitchen equipment, he tiptoed up the stairs and into the main part of the shop.

Now, where had that noise come from?

He had the impression that it was somewhere in the direction of the Gentlemen's Outfitting Department.

Creeping through the dark, with his sinister black bag in one hand and the knife held high in the other, he made his evil way across the floor.

Meanwhile, in the street outside, the New Cut Gang were rapidly changing their plans.

'He's dead,' said Zerlina. 'That horse-reviver's done for him. He's only an old man.'

'I think he's fallen over and broken his leg,' said Thunderbolt. 'Or his neck, maybe.'

'Stuff!' said Angela. 'He's fast asleep. I can hear him snoring from out here!'

'Never mind all that,' said Benny impatiently. 'We got an emergency here. Oh no! There's Jelly belly . . .'

Just turning around the corner, under the flaring lights of the Theatre, PC Jellicoe was moving majestically into the New Cut.

But as the policeman stopped to inspect the pictures

of the actresses outside the Theatre, Benny had an inspiration. He'd seen Thunderbolt fiddling absently with his lump of lead, and now Benny snatched it out of his hand and hurled it through the plate-glass window with an almighty crash. Glittering splinters of glass flew everywhere.

Before the others could react, Benny yelled, 'Mr Jellicoe! Mr Jellicoe! Quick!'

The constable had heard the noise and turned to look. When he saw Benny jumping and beckoning, he fumbled for his whistle.

'Hurry!' Benny yelled, and to the twins: 'Go and drag him – go on! Make him hurry—'

PC Jellicoe was breaking into a run, but he had to do it slowly by leaning forward and walking faster and faster. All the time he was trying to get his whistle to his mouth.

'*Peep-peep!*' came a feeble sound.

Thunderbolt ran to help. The constable lumbered up and stopped, heaving and puffing.

'Woss – goin' on? Eh? Oo – done – that?' he said, crimson and breathless, pointing at the window.

'Someone inside!' said Benny. 'We was just going past when there was this crash — someone's in there murdering people — look at the mess in the window!'

There was no denying that something awful *had* happened in that window. PC Jellicoe scratched his head.

'H'mm,' he said, still breathless. 'I better summon assistance.'

He felt for his whistle again, and turned towards the main entrance.

'Can I whistle for you, Mr Jellicoe?' said Thunderbolt.

'I reckon I got a bit more puff.'

'I think you're probably right,' said the policeman, and handed him the whistle before knocking loudly at the front door.

Thunderbolt filled his lungs and gave such a blast

that it nearly shattered another window.

And that was the sound that did for Mr Rummage. By this time he'd crept into the Gentlemen's Outfitting Department. Hearing the smash of the window, he'd almost lost his temper: how dare they! Vandals! He took a tighter grip on the 'Slysitoff' carving knife. Any burglar he caught would be lucky to escape without a puncture.

And then came Thunderbolt's blast on the whistle.

Police!

He'd have to hide the coins. Quick! Where could he put them?

He looked around in a panic, and had an inspiration: the 'Dux-Bak' dummy on the counter! The one old Paget had knocked over! One quick slice with the carving knife and he could tip the coins into its belly and have done with them.

He scuttled over to the dummy and held the knife high . . .

And of course it wasn't that dummy at all. Dippy had been snoozing peacefully, stretched out on the counter, but when he heard footsteps he opened his eyes.

And seeing a wild-eyed lunatic about to slice him open with a carving knife, he sat up at once and screamed at the top of his voice.

Mr Rummage was even more startled, if possible. To find a dummy opening its hideous eyes and sitting up and screaming at him was more than his nerves could take.

He dropped the knife, leaped six feet backwards and four feet in the air, and screamed even louder. The

Gladstone bag flew out of his hand and landed on the floor, where it burst open, scattering a fountain of coins everywhere.

And while Mr Rummage and Dippy were screaming at each other, the door burst open and in came PC Jellicoe, followed by a mob of howling children.

The shop was dark, of course, but Benny struck a match at once and lit the nearest gaslight.

'Look!' he said, pointing dramatically at the quivering Rummage. 'Guilt all over him, Mr Jellicoe!'

And holding the detective camera still, he took a photograph.

'Eh?' said the policeman. 'This is the shop-owner!'

'Look at these snide coins, Mr Jellicoe!' said Thunderbolt. 'Thousands of 'em! He's been uttering 'em! See? *He's* the one that did it!'

But all Mr Rummage was uttering now were the words 'The dummy – the dummy—' in a hoarse and broken voice. He pointed a quaking finger at the counter.

They all turned to look. There on the polished

wood, lying full length, was a plaster dummy wearing a 'Dux-Bak' mackintosh.

PC Jellicoe strode up and prodded it with a mighty finger.

'Well?' he said. 'Wot about it?'

'It sat up! Its eyes! Its face! Horrible! It screamed at me!'

Under the other side of the counter, unseen by anyone, Angela clamped her hands over Dippy's mouth while Zerlina whispered in his ear, 'Hush! Keep quiet, Dippy!'

Benny said loudly, 'It's clear what happened, Mr Jellicoe. Mr Rummage was going to hide all these snide coins what he's been passing out, and his guilty conscience got too much for him, and he had an illumination.'

'Hallucination,' said Thunderbolt.

'Yeah, one of them. You can tell he's had a shock. He musta been awful guilty. All them coins he's been passing out all this time . . .'

PC Jellicoe, still breathing heavily, turned over one

of the sixpences in his fingers and then bit it.

'H'mm,' he said. 'Was this in your possession, Mr Rummage?'

'Yes. Yes. I admit it. It's true. I'm guilty. I confess. The dummy – don't make me stay with the dummy – take me away—'

PC Jellicoe pulled out his handcuffs.

'I have no alternative but to apply the full rigour of the law,' he said. 'Roger Rummage, I arrest you for the utterance of forged coins . . .'

In the excitement, the twins managed to smuggle Dippy out of the shop. A crowd was beginning to gather, and once they realized what Mr Rummage had been arrested for, they became quite angry.

'Rich man like him taking money out the pockets of the poor!'

'He should be ashamed!'

'Oughter cut his head off, I reckon. If it was good enough for King Charles, it's good enough for him.'

'All right, all right, move aside,' said PC Jellicoe, guarding the shivering shop-owner. 'This man is my lawful prisoner, and I'm a-going to take him down the nick and charge him according to due process of law, so clear out the way else I'll fetch you a belt round the ear.'

No one wanted to risk a belt round the ear from PC Jellicoe's ham-sized fists, so they made way, and a procession followed them all the way to the Police Station.

At the head of it was Thunderbolt.

'Mr Jellicoe, they'll have to release my Pa now, won't they? 'Cause if you've got the real criminal, they'll see Pa's not guilty.'

'I can't be answerable for the decisions of the magistrate,' said PC Jellicoe loftily.

And the gang had to put up with that. When they reached the Police Station the crowd was shut out, but Benny and Thunderbolt were admitted as witnesses.

The sergeant on duty wrote down all the particulars, and looked very hard at Mr Rummage when he explained about the dummy.

'It sat up! It opened its eyes! It screamed at me! I can

see now that it was a horrible warning, Sergeant. I should never have given in to temptation. I'll never do it again. Oh, those eyes! Those hideous eyes!'

'H'mm,' said the sergeant, writing it all down.

And after Mr Rummage had been taken away to the cells, and the Gladstone bag and the coins and the 'Slysitoff' silver-plated carving knife had been locked away as evidence, the sergeant looked up to find Thunderbolt still waiting anxiously at the desk.

'You still here? Wotcher want? There ain't no reward, you know.'

'I want my Pa,' Thunderbolt said.

'That's right!' said Benny. 'You can't hold two prisoners for the same offence. It's against the law. And you know old Rummage done it, 'cause he said so. *And* I got a photograph to prove it!'

He brandished the detective camera pugnaciously.

'So can I have my Pa back?' said Thunderbolt.

'No,' said the sergeant.

The two boys opened their mouths and then shut them again. Thunderbolt suddenly felt very small.

'Why?' he said after a moment.

''Cause your Pa wasn't arrested for coining. He was arrested for another offence altogether, and he's been remanded on bail. Have you got fifty pounds to bail him out? I thought not. So what you going to do now?'

Seven

A Victim of the Spanish Inquisition

Thunderbolt just stood and gaped. Then he shut his mouth slowly and swallowed hard. Bail? Fifty *pounds*? And . . .

'What was he arrested for, then?' he said.

'Didn't they tell you, son?'

He could only shake his head. His heart was beating fast. The sergeant was looking serious, and Thunderbolt could tell from his expression that he was about to say something terrible – but he didn't, because there was an interruption.

Someone was banging and shouting. A voice he recognized – Bridie's – was raised in anger, and when Bridie raised her voice, the whole street knew about it.

The sergeant opened his mouth to protest, but another voice joined in. A foreign voice. A Frenchman's . . .

The sergeant and the two boys all turned to look as the door burst open. PC Jellicoe, who'd been outside arguing, was nearly knocked to the ground as Bridie rushed in, with Sharky Bob at her heels, and the mysterious Frenchman only a foot or two behind.

Her face was as red as her hair, and a beam of triumph lit her up like a lighthouse. She forced her way to the counter and slammed down a cotton shopping bag.

'I done it!' she cried. 'I found him!'

'Woss all this?' said the sergeant. 'Constable, what d'yer mean letting all this crew in?'

'She's got a ... relic, Sarge,' said PC Jellicoe, looking pale and nervous.

'A *what?*'

'A ... yuman 'ed,' gulped the constable.

Bridie scoffed, and opened the shopping bag to reveal the head of the waxwork Dippy. The sergeant recoiled in horror.

'What in the world—'

'It's made o' wax, ye great baboon!' she cried. 'Except it *isn't* wax! Thunderbolt, it's all right! Ye're rich, old feller! Tell him, Sharky!'

'It's *amblegrease*!' shouted Sharky Bob, joining in as Bridie whirled Thunderbolt in a jig.

And suddenly everyone was talking at once, including the Frenchman. But no one's voice was louder than Thunderbolt's, as he shouted:

'SHUT UP!'

'Just what I was about to say,' said the sergeant. 'You, girl, what's-yer-name, *you* talk. No one else.'

So Bridie breathlessly said, 'It was all them fellers trying to steal our waxwork. And Monsewer here, I didn't think he was a thief, but we never let him talk. And it got me thinking, and me and Sharky opened up the dummy and found nothing bar straw and old bits o' rubbish, so it had to be the head, ye see? And it was Thunderbolt's lump of wax! *Except* that I remembered his homework . . .'

And she spread out a filthy piece of paper on the counter. The sergeant read:

'*Ambergris: fatty substance of a marmoriform or striated appearance exuded from the intestines of the sperm whale, and highly esteemed by perfumiers . . .* What the blazes does that mean? Striated? Marmoriform?'

'Dunno,' said Benny. 'No one's gonna know till we get to S and M in the dictionary. We're only on A.'

'That's not important,' said Bridie impatiently. 'It's the perfume bit that matters. So I found Monsewer here, 'cause I reckoned that's what he was after, and I was right! I was *right*!'

The little Frenchman, who had been twitching with excitement, said, 'Yes! Mademoiselle is correct! I am Gaston Leroux, *parfumier*! I am the maker of the finest, the most exquisite perfumes and scents in the weurld! And when my *neuhse* – this organ so delicate and senstive' – he touched his nose with the fingertips of both hands, as if he was making sure it was stuck on properly – 'when my highly trained and irreplaceable *neuhse* caught the fragrance of ambergris, I followed it. Then I lost it. Then it followed *me*. This is the finest – the most profoundly beautiful piece of ambergris I have evair seen! I *meust* have it! My genius demands it!'

The sergeant rubbed his eyes.

'What d'you mean, you must have it? It belongs to young Thunderbolt here, by the look of things. If you want it, you'll have to buy it off him. What's it worth? A couple of quid?'

'More'n that!' said Bridie. 'Tell 'em, Monsewer! Go on!'

'Ah weel peh,' said M. Leroux with dignity, 'the market prahce for this. And that is six pounds per ounce.'

No one spoke. No one moved. No one could.

Finally Thunderbolt uttered a squeak.

'Six *pounds*? An *ounce*? But there must be . . .'

He goggled at the battered head, with its horsehair moustache, its blood-alley eye, its cracked and stained teeth. Then the sergeant blew out his cheeks.

'Where's them postal scales?' he said. 'Look sharp, Constable!'

PC Jellicoe handed him a little brass set of scales from the desk.

'I don't weunt the moustache,' said M. Leroux. 'Or the eye. Or those teeth. Ugh! Remove them!'

Benny dug them out, and the sergeant tenderly lifted the head onto the scales and balanced it with the little brass weights.

'I make that four pounds, fourteen and a half ounces,' the sergeant said. 'That correct, Monsewer?'

'Perfectly!'

Out came a notebook. The sergeant licked the point of his pencil and began to work out the sum, and so did M. Leroux, and so did PC Jellicoe. The constable gave up after a minute and waited for the other two to finish. Finally the sergeant showed his sum to M. Leroux, and they nodded.

'Four hundred and seventy-one pounds,' said the sergeant.

'Absolutely correct,' said M. Leroux.

'But . . . Sharky must've ate about fifty quid's worth!' said Benny, overawed. 'And old Ron the terrier – he ate the nose—'

And they all looked at Thunderbolt. First he went bright red, then he went pale, then he sniffed very hard and said, 'Well . . . Blimey. That's . . . That's enough to pay Pa's bail! I can get him out!'

'He's a lucky man,' said the sergeant.

M. Leroux paid some gold on account, and the sergeant offered to put the head in the safe until the cheque had cleared, so that everything was above board, and then PC Jellicoe took Thunderbolt along to the magistrate's to see about the bail. Thunderbolt was feeling so dizzy he could hardly think.

When the magistrate heard what it was about he said, 'Oh dear me, Mr Dobney, yes, I remember the case ... Dear dear! Out at last, is he? Bright spark, that fellow! Shocking case! Ha ha ha!'

Thunderbolt didn't understand it at all, and he was far too nervous to ask. Then there came another walk, to the prison in Renfrew Road, down past Bedlam where the poor lunatics were locked up.

PC Jellicoe saw Thunderbolt looking up at the great dark bulk of the hospital.

'Pity the poor fellers in there,' he said. 'Take more'n amblegrease to get *them* out.'

The Prison Governor took the magistrate's order and sent for a warder, who left the room jingling a bunch of keys. And much sooner than Thunderbolt had expected, there was Pa, in prison overalls, blinking and rubbing his hair. The Governor left them alone for a minute, and neither Thunderbolt nor Pa knew what to say.

Then Pa put his arms out, and Thunderbolt hurled himself at Pa and pressed his wet cheeks against his

father's chest, squeezing him round the middle tight enough to hurt. He felt he was hurting both of them: himself for ever thinking that his dear Pa could do anything as mean as forge money, and Pa for not telling him what he *was* doing, and himself again for being afraid to go to the police because of that silly lump of lead.

His father patted his shoulder over and over again, and ruffled his hair.

''S all right, old son,' he said. 'I'm free now. We'll get out in a minute and go home. Cor, I'm starving. They give us gruel in this place what tastes like wallpaper paste. And *you* ain't et for days, by the look of yer.'

'Mrs Malone's been looking after me,' said Thunderbolt, his face still muffled in Pa's chest. Then he let go, and while Pa got his proper clothes on, Thunderbolt blew his nose and wiped his eyes so they could both pretend he hadn't been crying.

They said goodbye to PC Jellicoe, and good riddance to the prison, and strolled along the midnight streets towards home. There was a coffee stall in St George's Circus, outside the Surrey Theatre, and they stopped and had a cup of coffee with two toffs in top hats, one sailor who was lost and two brightly painted young ladies.

'This is my son,' Pa announced. 'He's just sprung me out o' captivity. And in honour of my release, I'm going to stand coffee all round. Serve it up, my man, and raise your cups, ladies and gentlemen, in a toast to my son Thunderbolt.'

The toffs and the sailor and the young ladies all drank Thunderbolt's health, and he felt as proud as the Prince of Wales.

Later, when they'd got home and locked the door

and lit the fire to make some cocoa on, and Thunderbolt had told Pa all about the ambergris, he asked what he'd wanted to ask ever since the whole business began.

'Pa,' he said, 'what *did* they lock you up for? Was it to do with them batteries in the basement?'

'Yeah,' Pa said.

'Well . . .' Thunderbolt went on. 'What were you doing?'

Pa twisted his mouth under his moustache. Then he rubbed his hair again so it stuck out in all directions.

'It's a bit embarrassing,' he said. 'I didn't know how to tell yer, 'cause you might think . . . I dunno what you might've thought. It was electric ladies' corsets.'

'*What?*'

'Electric corsets for ladies with backache. See, I had this notion of a corset with wires in it, and a battery, and you could regulate – well, I don't mean *you*, I mean the lady – she could turn the current up or down and keep herself warm and ease the backache. Only the first ladies what tried 'em kept getting awful shocks, and it was costing me more and more to insulate it proper . . .'

He had to stop because he was smiling, and so was Thunderbolt, and then the thought of electrically heated ladies leaping in alarm with sparks flying out of their corsets was too much for them, and they burst out laughing.

'So I borrowed some money to cover it, and I couldn't pay it back . . .' said Pa eventually, wiping his eyes. 'Fizz! Crack! Hop!'

And that sent Thunderbolt off again. He kept waking up in the night and finding a broad grin on his face, so he knew he must be happy.

But the gang still had some unfinished business to attend to, and no one was more aware of it than Benny.

'We promised Dippy,' he said. 'We *promised* the old boy we'd get him in the Waxworks, and we ain't. Here! When's Monsewer coming back for the rest of the head?'

'This afternoon,' said Thunderbolt. 'The money's

cleared all right now, so the sergeant said he could have it any time he likes, and he's going to fetch it at three o'clock, he says.'

'Right,' said Benny. 'You leave it to me.'

And whatever Benny said to M. Leroux must have worked, because when the others came out of school that afternoon, Benny met them by the sweetshop, smiling proudly.

'Follow me,' he said, and led them round the corner to the Waxwork Museum.

Professor Dupont the proprietor welcomed them, to everyone's surprise, and showed them into his office, which was lined with shelves containing rows and rows of wax heads.

'Well, ladies and gentlemen,' said the Professor, 'my eminent compatriot M. Leroux has told me of the gallant deeds of our friend M. Hisspot.'

'Hitchcock,' said Bridie.

'Exactly. Well, in view of his great fame and valour, I am prepared to exhibit a figure of M. Twitchlock.'

'Hitchcock!'

'Just as you say. M. Leroux showed me the head you

made, and I must say I revised my opinion of your skill. In fact I have never seen so remarkable a work of art before.'

Benny was glowing with modesty. 'Yeah,' he said. 'I reckon I could do anyone. I could do Sexton Blake for yer— '

'We will stick to M. Fishdock for now,' said the Professor. 'What colour are his eyes?'

He opened a drawer full of eyes, and while the gang argued about the precise colour of Dippy's, the Professor took a second-hand head from the shelf.

'Take this wax,' he said, 'and make me a portrait of M. Hitchpot, and I will give it a place of honour in the Museum.'

So they took the head, and they chose some eyes, and they set to work.

Actually, of course, it was Benny who did the sculpting. He felt he had to redeem himself, because the picture in the detective camera, when it was developed, showed nothing but a murky glimpse of Benny's own stomach; he'd had it on back to front.

Still, that didn't matter, as Mr Rummage had confessed.

So he got to work, and life got back to normal. The twins were busy getting racing tips from the stable-boys in Hodgkins's Livery Stables, and Thunderbolt had to catch up with his homework. They'd got to C now: cataplasm, châtelaine, cochineal . . . As for Bridie, she'd fallen in love with Edmund Fitzwilkins, an actor at the Surrey Theatre, and she hung around the stage door, weak with longing.

Pa paid back the money he'd borrowed, and the magistrates let him off with a caution, once they managed to keep their faces straight enough to do so.

'No more electric corsets,' they said. 'Shocking idea.'

'Wouldn't dream of it,' said Pa.

So Benny worked alone; but being a genius, he didn't mind that. The others got hold of Dippy from time to time and dragged him to the hideout to model. He still felt a bit odd from the effects of the horse-reviver, but he didn't want to refuse in case they made him do something else dangerous.

And after three days of concentrated work, the

head was ready. Benny unveiled it proudly, and Dippy and the others stood around, dumb with admiration, almost.

'It's as good as the first one,' said Zerlina.

'It's better,' said Angela. 'More *passionate*.'

'It's a masterpiece,' said Thunderbolt. 'It's revolutionary!'

As for Dippy, all he could say was, 'Thank you, kids. Thank you. I can't hardly believe it . . .'

The Professor took it in with delight.

'Formidable!' he said. 'I shall do my best to provide a body worthy of this — this masterpiece! Truly it displays an imaginative vision the equal of Edgar Allan Peuhh . . . Leave it with me, dear boy! I shall make it the centrepiece of a display that will astonish the weurld! Come back on Saturday for the grand opening.'

So they did. Dippy went with them, naturally, with his best schmutter on and his hair stuck down with macassar oil. He looked a treat. Mr Dobney came too. There was a big crowd, thronging the Museum for a sight of the startling new exhibit. There were posters about it:

SEE THE ASTONISHING
NEW FIGURE!
Sculpted by an Eminent Local Artist
and modelled by a citizen of Lambeth

MR HICKY DIPSTOCK

the figure
BREAKS ALL BARRIERS
of expressive realism
and
SETS NEW STANDARDS
OF ARTISTIC ASTONISHMENT
IN THE BASEMENT
—— NOW! ——

'The basement?' said Benny. 'That's the Chamber of Horrors, innit?'

They hurried down the dark narrow stairs and into the dimly lit, brick-vaulted, cobwebbed dungeon that housed the worst horrors the Wax Museum offered. A notice said:

> ## A PRIZE OF £5 WILL BE OFFERED TO ANYONE WHO CAN STAY IN THE CHAMBER OF HORRORS OVERNIGHT!

and underneath was added:

> ## IN VIEW OF THE
> # POWER
> ## AND
> # GRUESOMENESS
> ## OF THE NEW DISPLAY, THE PRIZE IS RAISED TO £10!

The gang's eyes swept over the scenes of murder and carnage that lined the walls – throats being cut, heads being chopped off – they'd seen it all before. But in one corner an excited crowd was buzzing with chatter, and as the kids looked, two people had to be helped away pale and shaking.

'Where is it?' said Benny. 'What've they done with my masterpiece?'

He shoved his way through the crowd, the others close behind. Then they stopped by a sign that said:

A VICTIM OF THE
SPANISH INQUISITION

Lit by a flickering torch was a scene from a dungeon: a priest, a black-masked torturer wielding a red-hot pair of tongs, and cowering on the floor in rags, a poor shivering figure with the head of Dippy Hitchcock, as modelled by the eminent local artist Mr Benny Kaminsky.

It was exactly as Benny had made it. Not a bit had been changed, but somehow, in these surroundings, it expressed a hideous, nameless fear, enough to give anyone nightmares. The rolling eyes — the lips drawn back in a cry of anguish — every line of the poor tormented face spoke of despair and horror.

'H'mm,' said Benny. 'It never looked like that in the hideout.'

'It's good though, Dippy,' said Mr Dobney.

And the people around seemed to agree.

'Look at the suffering in his eyes!'

'I can't bear to look at it . . .'

'They must've done things to him what was too horrible to contemplate!'

'He must of been through mortal agony . . .'

And that, thought Dippy, was not very far from the truth.

The
Gas-Fitters'
Ball

Contents

One

The Love Phoby

There was a terrible shortage of crime in Lambeth in the summer of 1894, and the New Cut Gang were lamenting the fact, loudly.

'Dunno what's got into 'em,' said eleven-year-old Benny Kaminsky, hurling his penknife for the twentieth time at one of the timbers in the stable-loft, and missing for the nineteenth. 'Seems to me they lost all their gumption, them crooks.'

'Maybe they've reformed,' suggested Thunderbolt Dobney, shoving up his glasses with a dirty forefinger. Thunderbolt was a tender-hearted youth a little younger than Benny, always willing to think the best of anyone. 'They might've given up crime and taken to market-gardening or summing. Like old Dippy gave up picking pockets.'

'He never really picked anyone's pocket,' said Angela Peretti. 'He made out he was a pickpocket to impress people.'

'Only no one was impressed,' pointed out her twin, Zerlina.

The twins were a year or two younger than Benny and Thunderbolt. Being girls, they would normally have had no place in a gang of desperadoes, except that everyone around the New Cut feared them superstitiously. Even Crusher Watkins of the Lower Marsh Gang had a healthy respect for them. They were small for their age, as pretty as angels, and so wicked they were hardly human; they were like a pair of dangerous spirits from the ancient Mediterranean, miraculously reborn in the dusty streets of Lambeth. Better to have them in the gang than out of it, said Benny, and the others could only agree.

Benny scowled and retrieved his penknife from the straw. 'Well, if someone don't do a robbery or a swindle or a murder soon,' he said, 'we might as well give up being detectives altogether. There's no future in it. Might as well take to begging. Might as well starve.'

It was July, and hot heavy weather. Everything was lethargic, from the water in the Metropolitan Drinking Fountain to the sweep of the old horse Jasper's tail, brushing away the sleepy flies in the stable below the New Cut Gang's hideout. And half the gang were off visiting cousins in Ireland or uncles in Manchester; and even the criminal world seemed to have packed its bags and gone on holiday. No crime! It was a dismal prospect.

Benny took aim once more at the post and flicked the knife at it. He was being a Gaucho Knife Artist, like the Amazing Gonzales, whom he and Thunderbolt had seen at the Music Hall the week before. Señor Gonzales (whose name, when Benny pronounced it, rhymed with Wales) had a beautiful assistant called Carmencita, whom he tied to a board and hurled a dozen wicked-looking knives at with stupendous force. When the assistant was untied, there was her outline in knives. Señor Gonzales then repeated the stunt, but blindfold, and with Carmencita spinning around so fast on a revolving board that she seemed to have ten heads and twenty feet. Naturally, this was a trick that Benny could have done just as easily, if he had the knives and the assistant; but with his one flimsy penknife, and with neither of the twins willing to oblige, what could he do?

The world was against him. Moodily he flung the knife, and once again it bounced off and buried itself in the flea-infested straw under the eaves.

'Well, we got Dick to meet Daisy in the park,' said Angela. 'So *that's* summing useful done.'

Thunderbolt and Benny perked up at once. They could win money on this.

'Is he gonna do it?' said Thunderbolt excitedly. 'Is he gonna propose?'

Dick Smith was a young gas-fitter, popular in the New Cut for his prowess as a cricketer, and Daisy Miller was a pretty young woman who everyone agreed would make the ideal bride for Dick. As a matter of fact, Dick thought so too; and so did Daisy.

The trouble was, Dick was too shy to ask her, and this had led the sporting citizens of the New Cut to make several bets on whether he would or not. Snake-Eyes Melmott, the local bookie, started by offering six to four against a marriage, and found some takers at those odds; but Dick couldn't bring himself to propose to her, and Daisy was getting impatient, and soon the price lengthened to two to one. And at those odds, sixpence would win a shilling, and Benny and Thunderbolt found themselves strongly tempted to back Dick to propose, for they had a secret source of information.

And that was the Peretti twins. Angela earned a

shilling or two by helping out at the Smiths', and Zerlina did the same at the Millers', so they had Dick and Daisy well under control.

'They're going to meet in the park?' said Benny. 'When?'

'Six o'clock,' said Zerlina. 'We told 'em to. He's bound to propose soon. He might do it today, if he can get his courage up.'

'How much did you bet with old Snake-Eyes?' said Angela.

'Half a crown,' said Benny.

'I bet a shilling,' said Thunderbolt. 'I wish I'd had a bit more. We can't lose!'

'I reckon we ought to get down the park and encourage him,' said Benny. 'It's—' He lifted one of the loose tiles and peered through the roof at the clock on the jeweller's opposite. 'It's nearly half-past five now. Come on! Let's go and cheer him on!'

The park was a scruffy patch of grass, muddy in winter and dusty in summer, set about with a few dozen trees, a bandstand, and a pond on which swam a family of depraved and malevolent ducks. Once, when Benny and Thunderbolt and Danny Schneider (currently visiting the uncle in Manchester) had paddled across the water in a tea-chest to the six-foot-square island in the middle, in order to set up camp and live off the wildlife, the ducks had fought them off with such passion that Benny still had a scar on his knee. And then the evil birds had sunk the tea-chest, so the gang had had to wade ashore covered in shame, to the immense amusement of their deadly rivals, the Lower Marsh Gang. Ever since then, Benny had stayed clear of the ducks, and treated all mention of them with disdain.

'Ducks?' he'd say. 'Oh, is there ducks on the pond? I never noticed. I don't think much to ducks.'

Luckily, Dick and Daisy were going to meet on a bench by the bandstand, nowhere near the pond.

'There's a great big bush just behind,' said Angela. 'We could hide in that and whisper to him what to say next.'

'Well, she'd hear as well, wouldn't she?' said Benny. 'She'd think it was a bit funny being proposed to by a talking bush. We better keep out the way. We'll watch from the bandstand, and then when he kisses her we'll go and get his signature on a piece of paper proving he asked her to marry him, and then go straight off and find Snake-Eyes Melmott. Two to one! I'll have seven and sixpence, with me stake money back!'

'I'll have three bob,' said Thunderbolt.

'They *do* kiss 'em, don't they, when they've proposed?' Benny asked, just to be sure.

'Sometimes even before,' said Angela.

'Sometimes more before than afterwards,' added Zerlina.

'Anyway, it'll be easy to tell,' said Benny.

So the gang hung about the bandstand, swinging on the rails, hurling sticks onto the roof, clambering around the outside without their feet touching the ground, and so on, all the time keeping one eye out for the park-keeper and the other on the bench where Dick was going to meet Daisy.

They didn't have long to wait.

Dick, dressed in his off-duty best striped suit and clutching a wilting bunch of violets in a trembling hand, arrived at the bench at five to six. His warmest admirers wouldn't have called him handsome, but he was a cheerful, friendly, honest-looking chap, and as brave a batsman as ever faced a bouncer; but today he looked pitiful. He kept running his finger around inside his collar, and fanning himself with his straw boater, and biting his fingernails.

'He looks like the prisoner in 'The Primrose Path, or If Only He Had Known', just after they condemned him to death,' said Thunderbolt. 'Me and Pa saw it last week.'

'Sssh!' said Benny. 'There's Daisy, look. I mean *don't* look.'

Daisy Miller was the prettiest young woman in the New Cut: everyone said so. She looked especially fetching on this warm summer evening, in a floral dress and a big hat with cherries on it, and the way her eyes lit up when she saw Dick made the New Cut Gang think that their bets were as good as won.

Little by little the kids stopped what they were doing and shuffled closer to the bench to listen.

'Hello, Dick!' said Daisy. 'Fancy meeting you here.'

'Yeah,' said Dick. 'Imagine that, eh? Ha! Cor.'

'Oh, you got some flowers, Dick! They look half dead.'

'They're for you, Daisy,' he mumbled, and shoved them at her like a saucepan he'd just discovered behind the stove with last month's stew in it.

'Oh, Dick! They're beautiful! I better get 'em in some water, else they'll snuff it,' she said, taking them graciously. 'Shall we – er – shall we sit down, Dick?'

He gulped.

'Er – yeah. Might as well, eh?' he said finally.

Daisy sat on the bench, and smiled nicely at Dick. He perched uncomfortably on the very end and stared hard into the middle distance.

By that time the kids were all behind the bush,

frankly mesmerized. Benny saw a vision of his seven shillings and sixpence: a fortune, to be spent on icecreams and ginger snaps for weeks to come. Thunderbolt (a sentimental soul) was looking forward to the kiss. As for the twins, they were burning to defeat Snake-Eyes Melmott; so they were all willing Dick to move closer to Daisy, and above all, *say* something to her. He seemed to be in a trance.

Daisy sat and twiddled the violets. Then she twiddled the cherries on her hat.

'Dick,' she said, and he jumped.

'Er – yeah?'

'You can sit a bit closer, Dick,' she said, and patted the bench.

'Oh. Er . . . Right.'

He moved an inch closer. Then he fanned himself with his hat. Then he took out a handkerchief and mopped his forehead.

'Dick?' said Daisy.

'What?'

'Aren't you going to talk to me?'

He gulped loudly. 'We – er – I – er—' He ran his fingers around inside his collar again. 'Daisy, I – er—'

'Yes, Dick?'

'I was wondering if – umm—'

'Yes?'

He gulped. 'Daisy, we got a new kind of fitting in today,' he said desperately. 'At the works. A new – umm – fitting.'

'A what?'

'A fitting. A gas fitting. It's called Wilkins' Excelsior New Improved Patent Self-Adjusting Pressure Tap. It's got two kinds of outlets, see, so you can have high-pressure for cooking and low-pressure for lights.'

'Oh,' she said. 'That's nice. But Dick—'

'Yeah,' he said. 'It's ever so good. What you do is,

you cut off the mains and get a two-way valve—'

'Dick!'

'– and then you put the rubber seal on the flange, and—'

'*Dick!*'

'What?'

'Do you love me or don't you?'

'*Eh?*'

He goggled at her, pale and sweating. Then he looked around for escape. The kids in the bush were nearly hopping with impatience.

'Say yes!' hissed Angela, and Zerlina clapped her hand over her sister's mouth.

''Cause if you don't,' said Daisy tearfully, 'I can't go on waiting, Dick, I really can't. 'Cause you know I – I— 'Cause you know Mr Horspath is – is— Oh, Dick! Honestly!'

And she stamped to her feet and swept away, leaving Dick to scratch his head in helpless despair.

'Who's Mr Horspath?' whispered Thunderbolt.

'He's the Deputy Manager at the Gasworks,' said Zerlina. 'He's courting her, and all.'

Dick, hearing her voice, turned around miserably.

'Wotcher, Dick,' said Angela, clambering out of the bush.

'Wotcher,' said Dick.

'What's up with Daisy?' said Zerlina.

The twins sat on either side of him. Thunderbolt and Benny thought they'd better stay in the bush.

'I dunno,' Dick said. 'I'd like to tell Daisy I love her, and all that sort of thing, and ask her to marry me, but blimey, whenever it comes near the point I get so blooming shy I dunno where put meself. And now Mr Horspath's courting her as well, I ain't got a hope. I might as well go and drown meself in the duck-pond.'

'She wouldn't like you then,' said Angela, thinking of what Benny and the others had looked like after their encounter with the ducks.

'It's not that I'm frightened,' said Dick. 'I'm brave all right. I could fight a lion, or anything. But I'm just too blooming shy . . . And there's the Gas-Fitters' Ball next week. If only I can get her to come to that I know I'll be able to propose, only I'll never get round to it now. I'm a failure. I'm a ruined man. I'm doomed.'

He groaned heavily.

'Why don't you take her to the Music Hall?' said Zerlina.

'D'you think that'd do any good?' he said.

'Yeah!' said Angela. 'Bound to. There's the Amazing Gonzales – he'd put you in the mood. And there's Orlando the Strong Man and Miss Dolly Walters the Clapham Nightingale. It's a good bill this week.'

'You might be right, kids,' said Dick. 'I suppose if she was enjoying the show and I asked her sort of casual-like to come to the ball, I suppose she might.'

'Bound to!'

The twins' confidence was uncanny. There was a great deal about the twins that was uncanny, in Dick's view; like many people, he found them even more disturbing when they were being helpful than when they were intent on mayhem.

'So we'll see Daisy and tell her, then,' said Zerlina. 'You be at the Music Hall tomorrow evening, and she'll be there, and as soon as you've seen the Amazing

Gonzales, ask her to come to the ball.'

'All right!' said Dick. 'I'll do it. Or I might do it after the Clapham Nightingale. Depends.'

'Just make sure you do,' said Angela darkly, and something in the way she said it made Dick think of assassins, and feuds, and bandits with long knives.

'I will, honest,' he gulped.

Thunderbolt and Benny came out of the bush. Dick had wandered away weakly, and the twins had chased off after Daisy.

'I reckon it'll work,' said Benny. 'It can't fail. You know what, we oughter set up training people to do things they're nervous about doing. Like suppose you had a cabman as was nervous of horses – we could train him to like 'em. Or a greengrocer as was frightened of cabbages. We could—'

'Frightened of cabbages?'

'You get all sorts of strange fears,' Benny explained. 'They're called phobies. I heard the itnertist talk about 'em – Dr Psycho – *you* remember. Him as itnertized old Dippy Hitchcock into thinking he was a chicken. You get spider phobies, and horse phobies and cabbage phobies, and all sorts. Dick's got a love phoby. Anyway—'

'But if a person was frightened of cabbages,' persisted Thunderbolt, 'they wouldn't want to be a greengrocer in the first place.'

'But if they *was*,' said Benny hotly, 'we could train 'em out of it, and then they *could* be one. Seems to me you don't *want* to help Dick. Seems to me you don't *want* to win this bet. You probably got a bet phoby,' he added severely.

Thunderbolt wasn't sure about that. He hadn't bet money very often, because Pa didn't approve except for sixpence on the Derby, but when he had (with the twins' advice) he'd generally been lucky. But then, the twins' advice was usually sound, and they'd advised him to put everything he had on Dick at two to one. It had troubled Thunderbolt a bit, though, because the shilling he'd bet with Snake-Eyes Melmott had actually been given him by Pa to pay for a trigonometry lesson, and if Dick didn't propose soon, Thunderbolt would be in trouble.

* * *

Trigonometry was a new craze for Thunderbolt. He'd become interested in it ever since reading about how the great detective Sexton Blake solved a murder mystery by using it to work out precisely what angle the sun had been at in order to shine through the magnifying glass and light the fuse that set off the dynamite attached to the kidnapped Brazilian heiress. Clearly trigonometry was essential in the detective profession, and luckily there lived nearby someone who could teach it to him.

This was Miss Honoria Whittle, the daughter of Mr Horace Whittle, the Chief Manager of the Phoenix Gasworks. Miss Whittle was a nice lady, Thunderbolt thought, and clever too, because she'd been to college and learned to be a teacher. She gave Thunderbolt trigonometry lessons once a week, on Thursdays, which (come to think of it) was today, and if he didn't hurry, he'd be late.

He said goodbye to Benny and raced off to the Whittles' house in Nelson Square, where Miss Whittle was waiting for him as usual in the dining room, with the textbooks all ready. She was a gentle-looking lady, just getting a bit faded, with soft blonde hair and soft blue eyes. She wasn't as pretty as Daisy, of course, but then Miss Whittle was really old, sixty probably, or maybe thirty, anyway.

'Hello, Sam,' she said, because he was only called Thunderbolt on gang business.

'Miss Whittle,' he said, 'd'you reckon someone could have a love phoby?'

'A what?'

'I mean Dick Smith, who's in love with Daisy Miller, only he daren't ask her. Benny reckons he's got a love phoby.'

'Ah! I think you mean phobia. Well, you could be right. I think I knew someone who had a love phobia,' she added.

'Was he in love with you?' said Thunderbolt, interested.

Miss Whittle coughed wistfully. 'Come on, Sam, let's do some work,' she said, and they began.

Thunderbolt was half anxious in case she asked him for the shilling, but she was too nice to fuss. When they'd finished the trigonometry, she gave him a biscuit

as she always did, and they talked about Dick and
Daisy. Miss Whittle was really interested. Thunderbolt
was itching to tell her about the bet, because perhaps
she might like to put some money on too. But he didn't.

That night one of Benny's wishes came true. He
wanted a crime to solve, and someone provided
Lambeth with a first-rate one.

The Worshipful Company of Gas-Fitters had
several valuable silver dishes and trophies and so on,
which they kept in a cabinet in Gas-Fitters' Hall, near
the Phoenix Gasworks. There were salt-cellars and
soup tureens and goblets and salvers, and the prize of
the whole collection was the Jabez Calcutt Memorial
Trophy for the Apprentice Gas-Fitter of the Year,
consisting of a solid silver gas-fitters' wrench mounted
on an ebony plinth and surrounded with silver laurel
leaves. Dick's name was on it, because he'd won it
when he was an apprentice. It was a real work of art.

And that night someone broke into Gas-Fitters' Hall
and stole the lot.

Two

The Swedish Lucifer

The news of the burglary was all round the New Cut before breakfast. Ordinary burglaries were one thing, but this was a bigger job altogether than pinching a sack of potatoes from the greengrocer's or a tin alarm clock from the pawnbroker's window. The Worshipful Company of Gas-Fitters was an important body of men, and Gas-Fitters' Hall was the most noble edifice in the whole of Lambeth, apart from the Archbishop's Palace and the Lunatic Asylum, anyway.

As soon as the kids heard about it they ran there at once, and found a crowd gathered outside, staring at four policemen who were pretending to look for clues.

'I hear as they drugged the night-watchman,' said Dippy Hitchcock, the hot-chestnut and baked-potato man. 'They slipped him an unknown Chinese poison in a cup of tea, and he fell asleep and never heard nothing.'

Benny and the others listened, enthralled.

'I don't know about that,' said Mr Myhill solemnly, 'but I'm given to understand that that silver's worth over ten thousand pounds.'

Mr Myhill was a bank clerk, and understood the value of money.

'Daft, if you ask me,' said Mrs Fanny Blodgett of the Excelsior Tea and Coffee Rooms. 'What do a lot of blooming gas-fitters want with ten thousand quid's worth of silver plate?'

The men turned to her, shocked.

'Mrs Blodgett!' said Mr Tate the pawnbroker. 'The Worshipful Company of Gas-Fitters is a most ancient and honourable charitable association, fit to rank with the Dyers, the Tanners, the Vintners, the Merchant Taylors, all the most noble City Livery companies. Of course they need silver plate. I'm surprised at you for thinking otherwise. I thought you was a woman of sense.'

Benny led the others away urgently down a little alley at the side of the building.

'This is the crime we been waiting for!' he said. 'I bet we can solve it. I bet the police can't. I bet Scotland Yard's baffled. I reckon it's an international gang, that's what I reckon.'

'Or pirates!' said Angela. 'Off a boat on the river. Bound to be.'

'I just hope we can solve it before Sexton Blake gets to hear about it,' said Thunderbolt.

'Well come on!' said Benny. 'What we waiting for?'

'Look at this,' said Thunderbolt. 'Here's a clue straight off.'

He pointed down at the ground. Because of the dry weather, there wasn't much mud about just then, but a leaking overflow pipe somewhere above had dripped onto the dust in the alley and created a churned-up patch of wet yellowish earth.

'If we find someone with that colour mud on their

boots,' Thunderbolt said, 'they're as good as guilty. Sexton Blake knows all the different colours of London mud. He's always checking boots and that. We oughter do the same.'

'And footprints,' said Angela. 'We could look for footprints in it.'

'Yeah!' said Thunderbolt. 'That's a good idea.'

'That's what I mean,' said Angela. 'And we could of, and all, till you put your great plates all over it.'

Thunderbolt looked down. She was right; he'd trodden everything into a swamp. If there'd been any burglarious footprints a moment ago, there were certainly none now.

'H'mm,' he said. 'Oh well.'

Benny was peering closely at a little window four feet above the ground.

'Here's a clue,' he said.

The others gathered round. Benny was pointing at a dent in the woodwork near the window-catch which looked as if it had been made by a jemmy.

'That's where they forced their way in!' said Benny. 'Betcher!'

'Yeah, could be!' said Zerlina.

Thunderbolt was peering at it closely. His glasses didn't always work when he hadn't cleaned them for a while, and it was hard to clean them anyway given the usual state of his handkerchief, so he couldn't see the little dent as well as the others could. He felt along the window-sill and found something else, though.

'Here's a drop of wax, look.'

The others demanded to feel it too. It was almost invisible, but their fingers could make it out all right.

'A little blob of wax,' said Benny. 'That's *definitely* a clue! He musta spilled it from a candle. And look — here's a lucifer!'

He had spotted a match lying at the foot of the wall, and stooped to pick it up. This was the real thing, and no error. A genuine criminal match, combined with a genuine criminal blob of candle-wax right next to a genuine criminal jemmy-dent — it was too good to be true.

'OI!'

The roar resounded down the alley, and all the kids looked up, startled. PC Jellicoe, the stoutest policeman

in the whole of Lambeth, was standing in the entrance.

'Get out of it! Go on! Move along there!'

Benny darted up to him, holding the match.

'Mr Jellicoe! Look what we found! It's a clue!'

'Oh, it's you lot,' said PC Jellicoe, recognizing him. 'Go on, hop it. This is a serious police investigation. What are you doing here anyway? You oughter be in school. Or prison. I know where I'd send yer.'

'But Mr Jellicoe—'

'Did you hear what I said? Clear off!'

'But we got a—'

PC Jellicoe's mighty hand, raised high, showed them clearly what they'd get if they didn't do as he said. They dodged past him out of the alley and stopped in the street to look back.

'No good telling old Jelly belly,' said Benny. 'It's the inspector we ought to tell. He'll know about clues and that.'

But the inspector was inside the building, and the constable on guard at the door was even less patient than PC Jellicoe. Benny had to move fast to dodge the automatic clout.

'Right,' he said hotly to the policeman. 'That's it. You done it now. When the New Cut Gang catches the burgular as done this job, you're going to look pretty silly. I wouldn't like to be in your boots. I wouldn't like to be a policeman then. I'd rather be a pantomime horse than a policeman when we catch the Gas-Fitters' Hall burgular.'

The policeman sneered, and Benny and the others left in disdain.

'You better not lose that match,' said Angela. 'Give us it here, I'll look after it.'

'Not blooming likely,' said Benny. 'Remember when you looked after Sharky Bob for the afternoon?'

Sharky Bob was the youngest member of the New Cut Gang, a cheerful, benevolent six-year-old who would eat anything, and often did. The twins had once borrowed him for an afternoon in order to match him against the Brixton Gobbler, an infant of similar talents, in a contest involving hard-boiled eggs. Sharky had beaten The Gobbler hands down, and the twins, who had bet a total of nine shillings on him, had run off at once to claim their winnings from Snake-Eyes Melmott. In doing so they'd forgotten Sharky Bob altogether. He was later found happily eating his way up the Lambeth Walk from chop-house to pub to baked-potato stall, followed by an admiring crowd, but the damage had been done: the twins had earned a reputation. They won bets, but they lost things.

They gave Benny a dark look, but he was intent on fumbling in his pocket for something to put the match in.

'Here it is,' he said. 'I'll keep it in me matchbox.'

He brought out a Bryant and May's matchbox and carefully slid it open. He had to be careful in case the unusual worm he kept in there had come alive again, but it was either dead or asleep. The worm was unknown to science, Thunderbolt said, but then, after three weeks in Benny's pocket, probably not even its mother would have known it.

Benny prodded the worm carefully aside and put the match in the box. Or tried to.

'Here,' he said, 'it won't go.'

The match was too long for the box.

'I thought all matches was the same?' said Zerlina.

'Give us a look,' said Thunderbolt.

He held it close to his eyes. It looked like every other match he'd ever seen, except that it was, now he looked at it, a bit longer than most.

'This is an even better clue!' he said. 'A highly unusual match!'

'Yeah!' Benny said, excited. 'That's right! Let's go and ask Mr MacPhail about it. He'll know all right.'

MacPhail's was the tobacconist's at the corner of the New Cut. Mr MacPhail sold snuff and walking sticks

and Smokers' Companions as well as tobacco and cigars and cigarettes and things, so he was bound to know about matches.

'Aye,' he said, examining it through his pince-nez. 'Swedish, this is. Not a British lucifer. Swedish.'

'How d'you know that, Mr MacPhail?' said Benny. 'I mean, apart from it being long, and that.'

'Because o' these little marks at the end.'

They all crowded round to look. He was pointing at the unburned end. Thunderbolt, blinking and widening his eyes, could just see two little grooves pressed into the wood on opposite sides of the square stick a fraction of an inch from the end.

'When they make 'em,' Mr MacPhail explained, 'there's a machine that holds the stick by one end and dips it into a tank o' thick inflammable stuff. Then they pull it out again with a wee blob on, and that's the head, ye see, and they march the sticks aroond till the head's dry and then pack 'em in the boxes. A British lucifer's made the same way, only British lucifers is held by a different kind o' machine that makes a different kind o' mark. Look.'

He took a Bryant and May's matchbox from the shelf behind him and showed them a match. He was right: on this one, each of the four edges where the sides of the match met had been nipped in a little about an eighth of an inch from the end. It was quite different from the Swedish one.

'D'you sell Swedish matches, Mr MacPhail?' said Thunderbolt.

'No, son. Only British ones.'

'So who d'you reckon might be using Swedish lucifers round here?' said Benny.

'A sailor,' said Mr MacPhail. 'Someone in the timber trade, mebbe. Anyone who's been to the Baltic recently.'

'Or any real Swedes,' said Thunderbolt. 'Like S—'

Benny kicked his ankle to shut him up. 'Right. Thanks, Mr MacPhail,' he said, and they left.

Outside in the street, Thunderbolt rubbed his ankle and said, 'What was that for?'

''Cause you might warn him, you clot!'

'Warn who? Mr MacPhail's not the burglar, is he?'

'Warn Sid the Swede, of course! That's who you were going to say, wasn't it?'

'Well, yeah,' Thunderbolt admitted.

Sid the Swede was a local villain. He was a furtive and rat-like little man who always seemed to know where you could find a bit of mislaid fruit and veg, or someone who could change the markings on a horse to make it look as if it wasn't the one that was pinched from the stables last week.

'Betcher it ain't Sid the Swede,' said Angela.

'Yeah, me too,' said Zerlina. 'I betcher lots.'

'Give you ten to one,' said Angela.

You didn't bet against the twins, even at odds like that.

'Why not?' said Benny.

' 'Cause he's in chokey,' said Zerlina, 'that's why. He got caught last week nicking washing off old Mrs Pearson's line.'

'He got jugged for a month,' said Angela.

'H'mm,' said Benny. 'Well, that puts a different confection on things. Seems to me we'll have to go inspecting every blooming box of matches in Lambeth. Every time someone lights a cigar we'll have to pick up the match afterwards and see if it's Swedish.'

'And if they've got yellow mud on their boots,' said Thunderbolt, 'they're done for.'

So the gang split up to go looking for Swedish matches, yellow mud and ten thousand pounds worth of silver.

That evening, Dick was going to take Daisy to the Music Hall. The twins wanted to go along too, in order to supervise him, but their mother wouldn't hear of it. She looked up from the table where she was rolling out some pasta and her dark eyes flashed.

'What you tink a you do with that poor boy?' she said. 'You leave him alone! He's a nervous, he's a shy, he don't a want silly faces talking at him to a do this and a say that and all so on. You a pester him, I cut a your troats.'

She reached for the knife with a beefy flour-covered arm, and they fled. Mrs Peretti had been threatening to cut her daughters' throats ever since they could remember. It was just a sign of how fond she was of them, and they always liked to hear it, because it reassured them that everything was all right; but it meant that they'd have to give Dick some careful instructions if he was to face Daisy alone.

They guessed he'd be a little early, so they waylaid him outside the Music Hall three-quarters of an hour before the show began. He was walking up and down the pavement in the sunny evening chewing his nails and muttering to himself.

'What can I do, kids?' he said miserably. 'Look at me! I'm a shadow of a man! I wish Daisy was a heavy-weight boxer, and I was going to go three rounds with her. I wouldn't be half so blooming nervous. If only I could think of what to say . . .'

'That's what we've come for, you great goopus,' said Zerlina. 'Just listen and we'll tell you what to do.'

'Now what ladies like,' said Angela knowledgeably, 'is flattery. You gotta tell her that her eyes is like stars.'

'And her lips is like cherries,' added Zerlina.

'Cherries? You sure?' said Dick.

'That's right. And altogether she looks like a fashion plate.'

'What's a fashion plate?'

The twins weren't sure themselves, but they had an

answer; they had an answer for everything.

'It's a special ladies' thing,' said Angela. 'That'll please her, you watch. Then in the interval you buy her an orange.'

'And in the second half you whisper, "Daisy, will you do me the honour of being my guest at the Gas-Fitters' Ball?"'

'And she'll say, "Oh, blimey, Dick, not half."'

'And you say, "Cor, Daisy, I love yer," and—'

'Here she is!'

The twins fled before Daisy could see them. They were like little demons, thought Dick nervously; one second they were here, whispering mischief, the next they'd vanished. And here was Daisy, looking prettier than ever.

'Hello, Dick,' she said sweetly.

He gulped so hard he nearly swallowed his own head.

'Hello, Daisy,' he croaked.

Should he start flattering her straight away? Or should they get inside first? Luckily, the queue was moving forward, and he didn't have time to say anything until he'd bought the tickets and they were sitting in the middle of the stalls. He helped her in and sat down beside her. The band was tuning up in the orchestra pit, the stage curtain was glowing crimson in the limelight, the gilt on the plasterwork was glittering, the boxes and the balcony were all full of jolly-looking people laughing and chattering. Dick looked around desperately, but there was nothing for it; he'd have to talk to her.

What on earth had the twins told him to say? It had gone right out of his head.

'Er—' he began.

'Yes, Dick?'

'Er – you look like a bowl,' he said.

'What?'

'I mean a plate.'

'A *plate*?'

'Yeah. Or a dish. I mean—'

What Daisy might have said in reply he never knew, because the band struck up with 'Down at the Old Bull and Bush', and she turned away bewildered, to look at the stage as the curtain rose.

During the first half of the bill, they watched Mr Hosmer Simpkins, the Lyrical Tenor; Madame Taroczy's Hungarian Spiral Bicycle Ascensionists; Mr Paddy O'Flynn, the Jolly Wee Man from the Emerald Isle; and the Louisiana Banjo Playboys. In between each act, Dick turned to Daisy and began to speak, but the chairman always spoke louder, and the audience roared with laughter at his jokes, and Dick had to open and shut his mouth like a fish.

At last there came the interval.

'I liked the Spiral Hungarians, Dick,' she said. 'Didn't you?'

'Yeah, I did, yeah,' he agreed. 'Cor. Here, Daisy . . .'

'Yes, Dick?'

'Umm——' he began. He was trying to remember the other things the twins had told him to say. Wasn't there something to do with the night and the sky? 'Your face,' he said nervously.

'Is there something on it?'

'It's like the – the moon.'

'The *moon*?'

'No, no – that wasn't it. Umm——'

People in the row behind were listening, and enjoying it all immensely. Dick mopped his forehead with a red spotted handkerchief. Perhaps he should have gone back to saying she was like a bowl, only that hadn't come out right, either. But the word bowl made him think of cherries, and then he remembered.

'Umm – your eyes is like cherries, Daisy.'

'What d'you mean, Dick? Are they bloodshot or something?'

'No,' he said. 'No. Not at all. No. What I mean is, your lips. That's what I meant. Like – umm—' This was awful, he thought. He'd forgotten it altogether, but he had to go on now he'd started. Fruit; some kind of fruit; come *on* . . . Oranges, was it? No; couldn't have been. 'Bananas,' he said desperately.

'Why?' she demanded.

He hadn't the faintest idea.

'Er – same shape,' he mumbled doubtfully.

'What *do* you mean?' she said. 'Honestly, Dick, if I didn't know you better, I'd say you was trying to upset me.'

'Oh, Lor – no – I'm not, honest—'

The people behind were laughing and nudging each other and telling the people in the next row back. More and more of the audience were trying to listen, craning over from the balcony above, peering at them through the opera-glasses.

Someone up in the seats behind yelled, 'Go it, Dick! I got five bob on yer!'

Dick looked round, puzzled, because he hadn't the faintest idea what the man meant, of course. Someone else took up the cry, and soon the whole audience was cheering like a racehorse crowd. As for Daisy, she was mortified, poor girl.

'I can't sit here and be laughed at, Dick, I really can't!' she said. 'It's awful! It's just too embarrassing for words! Everybody's listening, and I'm sure you mean well, but—'

And she stood up and struggled to get out along the crowded row of seats. A big groan of disappointment went up. Dick struggled after her, but he was too late; and then the band struck up for the second half of the bill, and the lights went down, and she was gone.

* * *

Meanwhile, the twins were pestering their big brother Alfredo to look out for Swedish matches, as the gang were doing. Alf was a hokey-pokey man, an ice-cream vendor, and naturally, spending his time in commerce, he was bound to meet a lot of men who smoked and dropped the matches in the street. So the twins said, anyway.

'D'you mean every time I see some bloke light up a gasper I got to get down on me hands and knees and pick up his dead lucifer? Get out of it!'

He was combing his thick black moustache and smoothing down his glossy black hair in the kitchen mirror, and he was dressed up to the nines.

'Where you going, Alf?' said Zerlina.

'I'm off to see my mate Orlando down the Music Hall. I got a special pass to go in the Stage Door.'

'Orlando the Strong Man?' said Angela.

'Yeah. He bought five pound of ice-cream off me the other day and swallered it just like that. He's a real gentleman. He's the strongest man in the world, I shouldn't wonder.'

'Can we come with yer?'

'Don't see why not, as long as you come straight back.'

So the twins set off with Alf, hoping they might be able to find out how Dick was getting on. They liked going about with their big brother; he was smart and handsome and all the young ladies liked his flashing eyes and his jet-black whiskers, and he was usually good for a lump of hokey-pokey on a hot day, especially if he'd won a bet. He once bet Stan Garside the butcher a whole guinea at a hundred to eight that the Archbishop of Canterbury would come and judge the Elephant and Castle Cat Show. Naturally, Stan thought he was on a winner, but sure enough, His Grace the Lord Archbishop did turn up, and he was as nice as pie. It was the twins who'd done it. They'd just gone to Lambeth Palace, knocked on the door, and asked. When they wanted to be, they were irresistible – or supernatural, one or the other. Anyway, they got a lot of hokey-pokey that day.

They reached the Stage Door and Alf waved his pass at the old porter, who didn't even look up from his copy of 'Wild West Yarns', and then they were inside the Theatre itself.

It was a dark, busy place, smelling of glue and greasepaint, with music and bursts of loud laughter coming from somewhere else in the building. Performers in costumes were waiting in the corridors or coming out of the dressing-rooms, a group of stage-carpenters were sitting around a packing-case playing cards, and they all greeted Alf like an old friend.

In one corner of the wings, Orlando the Strong Man was warming up. He was wearing a leopard-skin costume that showed off his mighty muscles, and he had a gleaming bald head and a huge black moustache even bigger than Alf's.

'Wotcher, Alf,' he said, 'and who's these young ladies?'

'Me sisters,' said Alf. 'They come to say hello.'

While Alf went to talk to some of the chorus-girls nearby, Orlando bent down and very politely offered his forefinger to the twins to shake. His hands were too big to shake all at once. As Alf had said, he was a real gentleman.

'Are you the strongest man in the world, Mr Orlando?' said Angela.

'Probably,' he said. 'You seen the act, have yer?'

'Yeah!' said Zerlina. 'We liked the cannon-ball bit best.'

'Ah,' he said. 'That takes practice. You have to—'

But he couldn't say any more because, to everyone's surprise, the curtain nearby swirled open and suddenly there was Daisy. She looked as if she'd been crying.

'Daisy!' said Zerlina.

'What's the matter?' said Angela.

'I – I got lost,' Daisy sniffed. 'I was trying to find me way out and – and—'

'Excuse me, miss,' said Orlando, 'but you seem to be distressed. Can I help in any way?'

'That's very kind of you, Mr . . .'

'This is Orlando,' said Angela. 'He's showing us his muscles.'

'He's got ever such a lot,' said Zerlina.

'Cor,' said Orlando, 'you ain't wrong. Here – look at this.' He struck a pose and flexed his mighty arms. 'You see that muscle there?' he went on, frowning at a spot behind his shoulder.

'Which one?' said Daisy. 'There's hundreds.'

'That one going in and out.'

'There it is!' said Zerlina, pointing.

'Oh yes! I see it now,' said Daisy.

'Well,' said Orlando, 'most people ain't got one of them.'

'Oh,' said Daisy, impressed. 'What does it do?'

'Well, it goes in and out,' said Orlando. 'Here! Did you know I can lift a full-grown ox in my teeth?'

'No! Really?'

'Yeah. The trick is to get it right between the shoulder-blades. You probably wouldn't be able to do it at first. I should practise on a dog if I was you, and work up to a calf. You seen the act?'

Daisy shook her head and dabbed her eyes with a little handkerchief.

'I was going to,' she said, 'but I had to leave.'

'The best bit is where they bounce fifteen cannon-balls off me head, one after the other. The trick is to get 'em right there,' he added, pointing at the middle of his gleaming forehead, 'else it could be dangerous. Anyway, miss,' he said politely, 'I got to go now, 'cause I'm on in a minute. I'm very glad to have made your acquaintance.'

He held out his hand, but as she was about to shake it, he took it back.

'No,' he said, 'I better not shake your hand. Shall I tell you why?'

Daisy nodded, surprised.

''Cause this hand can crush rocks,' he said. 'I got to be careful what I do with it. Goodbye, miss, and cheer up, eh?'

Then there was a roll of drums, and he sprang onto the stage to a great round of applause. The twins would have liked to watch, but there was Daisy to look after; things didn't seem to be going very well for the great bet. They took her out and tried to find out what had happened.

Oddly enough, Benny and Thunderbolt were doing the same thing at that very moment, with Dick. He had tried to follow her out of the Music Hall, but had taken a different turning, and run into the boys outside the foyer. They were hanging about watching every smoker with grim suspicion. Every time a match fell to the ground they pounced, but so far they hadn't had any luck.

'You seen Daisy?' Dick said.

'I thought she was with you,' said Benny. 'Here! Thunderbolt! Geezer in the straw hat . . .'

Thunderbolt darted across the road and practically snatched the match out of the hands of a stout man who'd just lit a cigar. He looked at the match closely and shook his head in disappointment. Benny sighed.

'Woss going on?' said Dick.

'We're looking for Swedish matches,' said Benny.

'Oh,' said Dick. Probably collecting them, he thought, like stamps or something. He sighed even more deeply than Benny.

That reminded Benny of the bet, and with an effort he pulled his mind back to it.

'Here,' he said, 'I thought you was going to ask Daisy to the ball?'

'I was,' said Dick in tones of the deepest gloom. 'But it seems to me that every time I open my mouth, I say the wrong thing. I told her her face was like a bowl of bananas. At least that's what I think I said. I can't remember. It's all gone dark in me mind.'

'H'mm,' said Benny. He didn't know much about the language of love, but he didn't think that sounded like a compliment.

Thunderbolt darted back across the street.

'No good,' he said. 'It was a Bryant and May's. What's the matter with Dick?'

Benny told him. Thunderbolt whistled. 'A bowl of bananas?' he said, impressed. 'Cor. She ought to be pleased, anyway. Anybody'd be flattered by that.'

'You think so?' said Dick, cheering up a little. Maybe it hadn't been such a mistake after all. 'Here, them Swedish matches you're looking for . . .'

'Yeah?' said Benny eagerly.

'Well, I know who'd probably have some. I mean, being as he went to the European Congress of Gas and Coke Industries in Stockholm last month to make a speech.'

'Who?'

'Mr Whittle,' said Dick. 'I dunno what's bin up with him lately, neither. He's bin acting most peculiar. Almost as if he had summing on his mind. Still, I can't hang about here. I better go and look for Daisy.'

He kicked at a gloomy bit of straw on the pavement and wandered away, sighing. The boys looked at each other with bright speculation in their eyes.

'Mr Whittle . . .' said Benny. 'I wonder.'

'And – and Miss Honoria Whittle was unhappy when I went for me trigonometry lesson. She kept sighing and gazing out the window. I thought she was sad about me not giving her that shilling I bet Snake-Eyes Melmott, but maybe she was worried about her Pa. Same as I was about my Pa over the snide coins business. So maybe he *is* up to summing. Cor!'

'Well,' said Benny, 'there's only one way to find out. We'll have to detect him good and proper. Come on! Let's get going!'

When the twins heard what Dick had said to Daisy, they thought it would be a good idea to keep out of his way for a day or so, in case he thought it was their fault. They knew that other people sometimes found it hard to believe in their good intentions.

'We oughter wrote it down for the great clot to read,' said Angela.

'That'd look good, wouldn't it?' said Zerlina. 'Fishing out a bit of paper and reading to her. I dunno what we can do.'

'You can't help some people,' said Angela.

Shaking their heads over the futility of human endeavour, they went home. They were so preoccupied that they didn't see Daisy, at her front door, being stopped by a handsome young man with fair curly hair, who lifted his hat very politely and told her how pretty she was looking. The young man was Mr Horspath, the Deputy Gasworks Manager, Daisy's other admirer. It was lucky for him the twins weren't watching, or they'd have been there in a second, to get him away from Daisy at all costs. Snake-Eyes Melmott was taking a lot of money in bets on him, and Daisy's mother strongly approved of Mr Horspath, because he had nice soft hands, she said, like a proper gentleman, not great rough oily shovels like Dick's. There was no doubt about it, Mr Horspath was a serious threat.

Three

The Albatross-loft

There were some things that Benny had to do alone. He trusted Thunderbolt completely, but trying to make Thunderbolt less clumsy was like teaching a horse to knit, and this job needed care. As for the twins – he shuddered at the thought.

Anyway, the great detective Sexton Blake didn't always take Tinker his boy assistant everywhere he went. Benny read about Sexton Blake's adventures every week in the *Halfpenny Marvel*, and he didn't have a high opinion of Tinker. Tinker's main duties seemed to consist of running about with messages, of handing Sexton Blake his magnifying glass, and of getting hit over the head by crooks, and Benny regarded him with patronizing scorn. Tinker couldn't have solved the snide coin mystery, could he? The New Cut Gang had wrapped that up triumphantly.

No, in Benny's eyes, he was the boss, and the rest of the gang went where he led and did as he told them; though he kept his fingers crossed superstitiously in the case of the twins. There had been many occasions on which Benny had been tempted to jump on an omnibus and travel across the river to Baker Street, knock on the great detective's door, and ask his opinion, as one professional to another. And this was one. Unfortunately, according to the current edition of the *Halfpenny Marvel*, Mr Blake was at the moment chained up in the cellar of an evil slave-trader in Constantinople, with a bottle of acid eating its way through the rope holding shut a cage of half-starved, plague-bearing rats. Benny reckoned the great detective had his hands full for the moment, though no doubt he'd be free next week.

So he sat through supper that evening fuming with impatience. Cousin Morris had looked in, as he often did, and he and Benny's father sat at the table as the late evening sunlight slanted through the parlour window, arguing at enormous length about whether or not the late Duke of Clarence had been a good or a bad influence on gentleman's fashion. They could never agree on anything, Pa and Cousin Morris. Then Mr Schneider from next door came to join in the discussion, and Benny's mother and his elder sister Leah made sarcastic remarks about the vanity and fussiness of men compared to the restraint and modesty of women.

Benny got up at one point and said, 'Excuse me, but I got summing important to do—' and his father said, 'No! No! Sit down! It'll do you good to hear a proper intelligent debate!'

And Cousin Morris said, 'Benny, Benny! This is golden wisdom we're talking here! There's people as would pay money to hear the quality of argument you get at your father's table! Isn't that right, Mr Schneider?'

'There's plenty in Parliament as could wish for the eloquence and fluency what runs as freely and nourishingly here as Mrs Kaminsky's chicken soup,' said Mr Schneider gallantly.

Benny's mother, clearing the table, rolled her eyes at Leah and said nothing. Benny sat where he was until they allowed him to go, and then raced up to his room in the attic, where he got down to some proper detecting.

He thought that Sexton Blake would want another look at the match first, so he fished it out of the folded bit of paper in which he kept it for safety and scrutinized it fiercely through his grubby magnifying-glass.

The head was only just burned, which meant that the match had been struck to light it and blown out almost at once. You could light a cigarette like that, or a lantern, but not a cigar; they took longer. Some of the wood below the head would have been burned away as well. That was worth knowing, thought Benny.

What would Sexton Blake do once he'd found that out? Make a note of it, probably. Benny tore a page out of the back of his History exercise book and wrote:

CLUE NUMBER 1.
Sweedish match. Probly used for lighthing cigrette or candel.

Then he remembered something else, and wrote:

CLUE NUMBER 2.
Blob of wax on winder sill of burguled premmiss's. Probly from a candel.

In a frenzy of enthusiasm he went on:

CLUE NUMBER 3.
Dent like what a jemmy would make next to winder.

He thought about the yellow mud, but that wasn't a clue in itself. It would only be a clue if he saw some on someone's boots. Finally he wrote:

CLUE NUMBER 4.
Mr Whittle has been in Sweeden.

That made him wonder what Sexton Blake would do about Mr Whittle. What he'd probably do, Benny thought, was disguise himself, and watch him like a hawk. The criminal always returned to the scene of the crime — everyone knew that. So if Benny saw Mr Whittle slinking back guiltily to Gas-Fitters' Hall, he was as good as caught.

The trouble was . . .

The trouble was, Mr Whittle was a nice man. He always shelled out generously when Guy Fawkes' Day came round; he'd seen the New Cut Gang once playing a game of street cricket against the Lower Marsh mob, during one of their rare truces, and he'd rolled his sleeves up and joined in, bowling out Crusher Watkins with a cunning off-break; and he always had his suits made at Kaminsky's, despite being rich enough, said Benny's father, to go to Savile Row.

However, a detective's duty was to detect, and Benny couldn't shirk it. As soon as school was out next day, he told Thunderbolt what he was going to do, and gave him solemn instructions about the future of the gang if he didn't come back.

Thunderbolt gaped. 'D'you mean—'

'What I mean is, this is a secret and dangerous enterprise what could easily go wrong,' said Benny grimly. 'He could be the head of an international gang of desperate robbers. He could've been acting the manager of the gasworks just in order to lull everyone's suspicions. I bet he's just carrying on acting it for the time being till everyone forgets about the robbery, and then he'll be off to Monte Carlo to spend the money. Like as not Miss Whittle ain't his daughter either.'

'I think she is,' said Thunderbolt doubtfully.

'I bet she's really called Diamond Lou or Six-Gun Betsy. She probably done the robbery with him. She's probably got one of them little guns in her stocking, a derringer, like Madame Carlotta had in the last Sexton Blake. She's probably waiting for you to make a trigonometry mistake and she'll plug you. I bet she's killed half a dozen—'

Thunderbolt knew the signs; this was where one of Benny's fantasies was leaving the ground.

'But what you gonna *do*?' he interrupted.

'Foller him everywhere,' said Benny. 'Like a shadder. He won't know I'm there, 'cause I'll be in disguise. You watch.'

Benny's idea of disguise was a comprehensive one. Finding clothes wasn't too difficult, because his father's workshop was usually full of suits waiting to be altered or paid for. He'd managed to borrow a smallish one in a vivid check, which had been waiting six months for its owner to come out of prison, and which he was sure wouldn't be missed. It only needed the trousers rolling up nine inches or so and the jacket padding out with newspaper. The sleeves were a bit long, but he could always pretend to have lost both hands in a fight with a shark. To go with the suit he had borrowed a brown bowler hat from his sister Leah's young man Joe.

Once the suit was on, he set about colouring his hair grey with a handful of flour, painting on a vast and sooty moustache with a burned cork, and giving himself a hideous bright red scar from forehead to jaw. He turned his face this way and that in the broken little bit of mirror they had in the hideout, and which they normally used as a periscope, when it wasn't being a heliograph. He couldn't speak; he was lost in admiration.

'What's the matter?' said Thunderbolt after a minute. 'It's not so bad. You just need to—'

'You know what,' said Benny suddenly, 'I oughter go on the stage.'

'Like Four-Ball?'

Danny Schneider, the gang member who'd been condemned to a month in Manchester, was known as Four-Ball because of his juggling skills. There was no doubt that he'd be topping the bill at the Music Hall one day, but that wasn't what Benny had meant.

'No,' he said. 'Like Henry Irving. They oughter do a play about Sexton Blake, and I could play him. And then when he was tied up in a cellar or summing I could play Dr Skull, the mad scientist. Then when Dr Skull gets killed by one of the evil ape-men I could play a good ape-man and rescue Sexton Blake, and then I could play him again. And then—'

'But what are you going to do about Mr Whittle?'

With a mighty effort Benny frowned, shook his head, and brought himself back to the present.

'Eh? Oh, him. I'll just foller him after he leaves the gasworks. He's bound to return to the scene of the crime, 'cause they always do. Then when I see him do that, I'll make a citizen's arrest.'

Thunderbolt opened his mouth to point out that Mr Whittle was a leading member of the Board of the Worshipful Company of Gas-Fitters, and he was bound to be visiting Gas-Fitters' Hall before long anyway; but you couldn't argue with Benny, somehow. Thunderbolt watched his leader saunter off in his voluminous check suit, hitching up the trousers for the tenth time in twenty paces, pushing up the bowler hat from the bridge of his nose, a drift of flour trailing behind him, and felt nothing but honest admiration.

* * *

Dick came out of work in a savage mood. He'd been feeling cross all day, and late that afternoon he wrenched so hard at a Wilkins' Excelsior New Improved Patent Self-Adjusting Pressure Tap that he broke the flange and had to pay for a replacement, which didn't improve his temper one bit.

So when Angela and Zerlina saw him coming, they were glad they were in the company of their new friend, the Mighty Orlando. He was off duty, so he wasn't wearing his leopard-skin; he was looking very smart in a striped blazer and a Panama hat. He had stopped at Alf's ice-cream stall for a refreshing gallon of strawberry-and-vanilla, and the twins had been hanging about there too, and Orlando had kindly bought them a lump each; and they were strolling along together past the gasworks in the sunshine when Dick came out with a face like thunder. Orlando was big enough for both the twins to hide behind him, but they were too late.

'Wotcher, gals,' Dick said gloomily.

They looked at each other quickly. Perhaps he

wasn't cross with them after all.

'Wotcher, Dick,' said Angela. 'This is the Mighty Orlando.'

'He's a friend of ours,' said Zerlina meaningfully.

'And this is Mister Dick Smith,' said Angela to Orlando.

'How d'you do, mate,' said Dick, holding out his hand.

'Please to meet yer,' said Orlando. 'No – I won't shake your hand. Shall I tell you why?'

'Yeah, go on,' said Dick.

''Cause this hand can crush rocks,' said Orlando solemnly, pointing to his right hand with a left forefinger the size of a cricket-bat handle. 'Find a rock – go on. Any rock. I'll show yer.'

'No, I believe yer,' said Dick, impressed. 'Cor.'

Feeling a little safer now, the twins told Dick about meeting Daisy in the Music Hall the night before. Dick looked embarrassed.

'Yeah,' he said. 'I spose I must've got it wrong, all them things you told me to say. I spose Daisy'll never want to see me again. I spose Mr Horspath'll have her all to hisself from now on.'

And he sighed like a 'Thunderer' Pneumatic Drainage Pump, and sat down wearily on the edge of the nearest horse-trough.

'I knows how yer feel,' said Orlando. 'Mind if I join yer?'

Dick moved up to make room. 'You had love trouble as well, mate?' he said.

'Not half,' said Orlando.

The twins perched on the horse-trough and listened, enthralled.

Orlando fanned himself with his hat, and went on: 'Oh, yus. I was in love and all, same as you, only I could never work up the nerve to tell her. I done all kinds of things to please her, like tearing books in half and crushing rocks and bouncing cannon-balls off me head, but I could never come out with saying I loved her.'

'That's just the same as me!' said Dick.

'And by the time I found out what to do, it was too late. Fate had passed me by.'

'You mean you *did* find out what to do?'

'Oh, yus. I know what to do now all right. Only

like I say, it's too late.'

'So what is it? What's the secret?'

'The secret of love,' said Orlando, 'was told to me by a Spanish hacrobat in a circus what I worked in once. And he oughter known, 'cause he had six wives at least. In different countries, of course. What he said was, you take a deep breath, close your eyes, grab hold of her hand, and cover it with burning kisses. About a dozen, he said. Once you done that, you feel quite different. Telling her you love her's easy after that.'

'And have you tried it?'

'No, I ain't,' said Orlando, ''cause of my undying love for the lady what I never done it to in the first place.'

Dick was nodding. There was a strange light in his eyes.

'Take a deep breath . . .' he repeated.

'That's it.'

'Close me eyes . . .'

'Yus.'

'Grab her hand . . .'

'That's the style.'

'And cover it with burning kisses.'

'About a dozen,' said the twins together.

'And if you do that,' said Orlando, 'I guarantee you'll be able to ask her to marry yer, and she won't have no choice but to say yes, because she'll be bowled over by your passion. Try it and see.'

'I will!' said Dick. 'I'll do it! Ta very much, Orlando. I'm obliged to yer, mate.'

Orlando stood up to leave, and held out his hand to wish Dick good luck, but took it back before Dick touched it.

'Oh, no,' he said. 'Better not. This hand can crush rocks. Cheerio, Dick, and the best of luck.'

Meanwhile, Benny was prowling up and down opposite the gasworks entrance, waiting for Mr Whittle to come out. His disguise made him impossible to recognize, of course, and he was almost invisible anyway because of the cat-like silence and swiftness of his movements. Only two nervous horses shied at his appearance, and only half a dozen ragamuffins with nothing better to do jeered at this strange painted figure with the flapping sleeves and the immense bowler hat; but he ignored them majestically. He was a tiger stalking its prey, and tigers take no notice of jackals.

Finally, at five past six, Mr Whittle appeared. Benny pressed himself back into the shadows of the alley opposite the gasworks entrance, and watched with narrow eyes from under the brim of his hat as Mr Whittle stopped for a word with the watchman at the gate. The watchman touched his cap, Mr Whittle raised his cane in salute, and set off – towards Gas-Fitters' Hall.

Benny felt a thrill of excitement. Hitching up the trousers, which had started to unroll during the cat-like movements, and wrinkling his nose to keep the hat-brim up, he darted from the alley and crouched in concealment behind a dustbin, watching Mr Whittle like a hawk.

And so began a strange procession up Southwark Street, under the railway bridge, and left into Blackfriars Road. Mr Whittle sauntered along, looking the picture of innocence. You'd never think he was a desperate criminal. He raised his hat to Mrs Fanny Blodgett and Mrs Rosa Briggs, who were enjoying the evening sunshine outside Mrs Blodgett's Tea Rooms; he bought an evening paper from Charlie Rackett on the corner of Blackfriars Road; he even stopped for a genial word with PC Jellicoe.

But always behind him, darting from dustbin to horse-trough to cab-stand like a phantom of Vengeance, came the strangely garbed figure of Benny Kaminsky.

And with every step they got closer and closer to Gas-Fitters' Hall. When they were nearly there, Mr Whittle stopped and looked around, as if he were suspicious that someone might be following him. Benny was ready for that. He was only about ten feet away, and there was no dustbin to dodge behind, so he sauntered on past without making the slightest sign that he'd even noticed Mr Whittle.

Once he'd reached the bow window of the draper's shop a bit further along, he looked in it for the reflection of what was happening behind, and to his delight he saw Mr Whittle look around once more and step into the alley right next to Gas-Fitters' Hall. Benny could hardly contain himself, for that was the very alley in which they'd found the match.

Forgetting about the cat-like movements, he turned and pelted back to the alley at top speed, stopping just in time to peer round the corner first, in case Mr Whittle was waiting with a drawn revolver or a blackjack or a stiletto. But he wasn't. Instead, Benny saw his legs disappearing up a flight of iron stairs at the other end of the alley.

Almost yelping with excitement, Benny followed.

It seemed to be a kind of fire-escape. As far as Benny could see, it went right to the top, and he could hear the measured tread of Mr Whittle's boots ringing on the iron and moving up without a pause. He followed as quietly as he could, looking up all the time through the grille-like steps, and only twice fell over the unrolling trouser-legs. The second time, though, the bowler hat rolled off and nearly fell through the steps down to the alley below.

He grabbed it just in time and turned back upwards. Mr Whittle's footsteps weren't making any noise on the

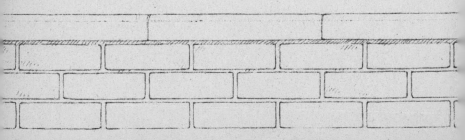

iron, and as Benny peered upwards through the gaps in the staircase he couldn't see the shape of Mr Whittle's body against the blue evening sky. Obviously he was lying in wait. Benny felt a tremor of apprehension. He tiptoed up the last flight of steps, which seemed to lead directly onto the roof. With enormous care he moved up until his eyes were level with the edge, and squinted from under the hat-brim with the hawk-like gaze of an Apache warrior.

The roof of Gas-Fitters' Hall was flat, with a little brick parapet around the edge. In the middle of it was a curious little hut, and outside the hut the great criminal was sitting on a wooden seat, stroking a pigeon which he held against his breast. A sound of soft coo-ing came from behind him.

'Hello, Benny,' said Mr Whittle.

'Er – I ain't Benny,' said Benny. 'He's – er – he's dead. I'm – er – someone else. Fred,' he said, inspired. 'Fred Basket.'

Somehow the second name wasn't quite as good as the first, but there was nothing he could do about it now. Mr Whittle removed his hand from the pigeon and held it out solemnly. Benny cautiously shook it.

'How d'you do, Fred,' said Mr Whittle. 'Sorry to hear about Benny.'

'Yeah,' said Benny. 'They're all dead, all his family.'

'Really?'

'Yeah. The – er – the roof fell in and squashed 'em. They couldn't even tell which was which, they was so squashed.'

'Dear oh dear,' said Mr Whittle. 'I shall have to go somewhere else for my suits now. That's a great pity. Squashed, you say?'

'Yeah. There was blood and guts and bones all over the place. But they could tell which one was Benny, just.'

'Oh? How was that?'

'They found him holding up the roof. Or trying to. He was holding it up so the others could get out. Sorta like this . . .'

Benny demonstrated someone of gigantic strength struggling to resist an overpowering weight on his shoulders. He staggered – he groaned – he sank to his knees – he tried to rise again, but finally fell with a piteous cry. The bowler hat rolled off and lay unnoticed by the door of the hut.

'A heroic deed,' said Mr Whittle. 'How did they know it was him if everyone was squashed, though?'

' 'Cause just his face was left, sticking out the rubble. Here, Mr Whittle—'

Benny was becoming more and more intrigued by the pigeon sitting placidly in Mr Whittle's hands. He scrambled up, the squashed Kaminskys forgotten, and came to look at it.

'– is that a carrier pigeon?' he asked.

'It's a racing pigeon,' said Mr Whittle. 'I've been a little worried about this fellow. He's been off his food, but I think he's better now. Would you like to see the others?'

'Cor, yeah,' said Benny.

'Hold this one, then,' said Mr Whittle, and passed it to Benny, who held it gently against his chest as Mr Whittle opened the door of the hut. 'I've always kept

pigeons,' Mr Whittle went on. 'I couldn't keep 'em at home, because they used to make my wife sneeze. When she died a few years back I suppose I could've moved the loft over to my house, but this arrangement seems to work pretty well. I pay a bit of rent to the Gas-Fitters' Company and everyone's happy. Here we are, then . . .'

The pigeon-loft was dark and warm and full of bird-like smells and noises. There was a row of neat little cages on each side, and about a dozen pigeons sat plumply on their perches.

'You want to help me feed 'em, Ben— er, Fred?' said Mr Whittle.

'Yeah!'

He took the pigeon from Benny and put it in its cage before giving Benny a little tin cup to scoop bird-seed out of a sack.

'About half a cupful each,' said Mr Whittle.

'Here, Mr Whittle,' said Benny, 'I bet you could train 'em to carry messages. They'd be a whole sight quicker'n the Post Office. Quicker'n a telegram, even.'

'I dare say,' said Mr Whittle.

'And *much* quicker'n a cab. You could have 'em flying all over London. They could deliver messages so quick you could make a fortune, probly. You could charge a penny a go. Or you could train really fast ones for threepence. Or you could train 'em to go and recruit other ones from Trafalgar Square! Or train a dozen of 'em to fly together and carry parcels . . . And every shop and company and factory could have a pigeon-loft on the roof and they'd have to pay rent for 'em like a telephone. Then you could start training some extra long-distance pigeons to fly to Paris and the Continent. And – and seagulls to fly to America. Or albatrosses, probly. You could have an albatross post office for across the sea and . . . Or even fish,' he said, completely carried away. 'You could train haddocks and that to swim with little waterproof bags. In a war that'd be dead useful, 'cause a haddock could go into an enemy harbour and take messages from a spy. You could train 'em to come to a special underwater whis- tle . . . Probly get a medal for it from the Queen,' he said. 'Distinguished Haddock Cross.'

'You probably would,' said Mr Whittle. 'Look, I'm going to close up now, because it's time I went home. It's been a pleasure talking to you, Fred. I'm only sorry about the Kaminsky family. What a tragedy!'

'Yes,' said Benny distantly. He was beginning to regret the falling-house story. 'Course, it might not have been them after all,' he added. 'They were squashed so flat, it was hard to tell. It might've been a different family, and someone who just *looked* like Benny's face sticking out.'

'Yes, it might,' said Mr Whittle. 'And there's a lot of people look like Benny, after all. You look a bit like him yourself. You be careful down those stairs now.'

He closed the door of the pigeon-loft, which had an ordinary latch and no lock, and the two of them went down the iron staircase to the alley. Mr Whittle turned to Benny, shook hands, and wished him good evening before strolling off. Benny watched him thoughtfully.

He might have been downcast, because Mr Whittle was plainly not the thief after all, so they had to start again. On the other hand, he liked Mr Whittle, and he was glad to find him innocent. Even the fact that he'd been anxious about something was clear now – he'd been worried about his pigeon; and if *he* wasn't the thief, then someone else undoubtedly was. And that was worth knowing.

He was about to go back to the hideout and get out of his disguise, which was getting hotter and more uncomfortable by the minute, when he suddenly realized he hadn't got the bowler hat. Of course! It had come off when he was acting getting squashed, and rolled behind the door of the pigeon-loft.

He scratched his floury head. His sister Leah's young man Joe had taken a lot of persuading to lend his hat, and Benny didn't fancy the trouble he'd be in if the hat wasn't returned in good time, and in good shape too, come to that. He'd have to go back up and get it.

He climbed the staircase again. Not wanting to waste the chance, he became an albatross-trainer climbing a wild cliff-face to the albatross-loft in order to send his fastest albatross on a desperate mission across the Atlantic. He struggled against the wild wind and the lashing rain, clawing his way to the rocky summit of the cliffs and crawling on his stomach across the storm-beaten grass in order to avoid being swept off. He reached the albatross-loft and hauled himself up, gasping with effort, and lifted the latch and fell full-length inside, panting.

The albatrosses shifted on their perches and cooed anxiously.

Benny lay there for a minute to recover from the

broken leg he'd sustained in a fall from halfway up the cliff, and then sat up, found the bowler hat absent-mindedly, and put it on. Time to feed the albatrosses, he thought. He gave each of them a haddock, and then rummaged behind the sack of bird-seed for the special waterproof message-pouch he was going to fix to the strongest albatross.

As his hands felt in the darkness he suddenly stopped and stood up.

Everything had gone silent and still. The albatrosses were forgotten. Benny's eyes, wide open, stared down past the sack of bird-seed as if they couldn't believe what was there.

Then he bent down again and carefully moved the sack away, and it was true, he hadn't dreamed it: behind the bird-seed was another sack, the top hanging open, and inside it was the faint gleam of silver. Great cups and bowls and plates, and in the middle a solid silver gas-fitter's wrench on an ebony plinth surmounted with silver laurel leaves. It was the loot from the robbery, and Mr Whittle had been hiding it after all.

Four

The Potted Palm

Benny shut the door of the pigeon-loft behind him and crept to the iron staircase, looking down to make sure the alley was clear. Seeing no sign of Mr Whittle, he cautiously climbed down, tiptoed out of the alley and ran away for the hideout as fast as he could.

He dodged through the stable, avoiding the automatic kick from Jasper the bad-tempered horse, clambered up the ladder, and found the hideout empty, to his relief. He took off the suit and rubbed his face on the lining of the jacket to get rid of the moustache, and succeeded, mostly. The suit itself was a little used-looking, mainly from being crawled across the roof in. He could brush it later, if he found a brush. The main thing was to get rid of the flour in his hair. It was no good washing it out; he'd tried that before, and the stuff turned into a very effective glue. For weeks afterwards he'd gone about with hair that made a light knocking sound when you tapped it, like cardboard, and mighty uncomfortable it was too, not to mention noisy. So he spent some time now shaking his head and running his fingers through his hair and rubbing it on the suit's trouser-legs until it was more or less its normal dingy brown again.

Then he prised a 'Monstroso' giant peppermint humbug away from the paper bag it was sticking to, wedged it firmly into his cheek as an aid to thought, and flung himself on the heap of straw in the corner to work out what to do next.

He hadn't been there long when the trapdoor lifted, and Thunderbolt peered in at him, looking excited.

'Here!' he said. 'Dick's gonna do it! He's got a love secret from Orlando the strong man, and he's gonna ask Daisy tonight! We're gonna win the bet after all!'

He clambered up, followed by the twins. Benny frowned austerely.

'And Snake-Eyes don't know about Orlando's love secret, so he's offering five to one against Dick now,' said Angela. 'It's worth borrowing a fortune for!'

'Imagine that,' said Thunderbolt, his spectacles glowing. 'Five shillings for a one-bob stake! Cor . . .'

'Mmm,' said Benny. He shifted the humbug from one cheek to the other, gazing into the middle distance.

'What's the matter?' said Angela.

'You ain't put some money on old Horspath?' said Zerlina suspiciously.

Benny gave her a cold look. Finally the others realized that he had something else on his mind, and remembered what he'd been doing.

'How'd you get on with following Mr Whittle?' said Thunderbolt.

Benny took out the humbug, balanced it carefully on one knee, and began to explain. He had never had a better audience; they sat wide-eyed and open-mouthed.

'You *sure*?' said Thunderbolt when he'd finished.

'You saw all of it? All that loot?' said Angela.

'It wasn't just tools for pigeon-breeding?' said Zerlina.

'You don't breed pigeons with gas-fitters' wrenches made of solid silver,' said Benny scornfully. 'Nor you don't need blooming great dishes half a yard across to feed 'em with, neither. I fed 'em meself with a little tin cup about *that* big. Mr Whittle let me do it.'

'But why would he let you do that if there was all that loot stashed behind it?' said Thunderbolt. 'It's funny him letting you in there at all.'

'That's what I think,' said Benny. 'But I tell you one thing, I got a plan coming. I can feel it. I just need to work out the details. But it's a good 'un. It's one of the best I ever had. In fact, it's a blooming cracker.'

Thunderbolt looked at the twins, who looked apprehensively back at him and then at each other. They knew the signs. Benny's eyes were remote, as if he were staring at something too far-off for the others to see, and his lips were moving faintly.

'Yeah,' he said after a minute or so, detaching the humbug from the dusty fibres of his trouser-leg before tossing it into the air and catching it in his mouth with a gulp. 'This is gonna be a stunner. It's gonna be a corker. It's gonna be a knock-down sockdologer!'

'But—' Thunderbolt began.

Benny held up his hand. 'I need to get it right first. Get all the details straight. You better leave me alone for now, else I'll get it wrong. I need silence and being alone. Go on, hook it. I'll find yer when I've got it all worked out.'

'You don't want to put summing on Dick at Snake-Eyes's five to one?' said Angela, halfway out of the trapdoor.

'No. I got nothing left anyway. Go on, I mean it, I want to think about it on my own.'

So the others left. Benny heard Zerlina enthusiastically explaining to Thunderbolt on the way down that if he placed his next trigonometry shilling with Snake-Eyes Melmott as well as the first one, he'd have a total profit of seven shillings when Dick finally triumphed. Her eager voice died away as the others went out through the stable, and then there was silence, broken only by the continual buzz of flies around old Jasper below, the swish of his irritable tail, and the high-pitched, almost electrical hum that Benny felt must be coming from his mighty brain at full stretch.

Daisy had been puzzled and a little hurt by the fact that she hadn't seen Dick since the unfortunate incident in the Music Hall. She understood what had happened; the poor boy had got his words mixed up. It wasn't his fault he wasn't a smooth-tongued genius. But she couldn't wait for ever, and meanwhile Mr Horspath was being so charming and attentive . . . He had brought her a box of chocolates the day before, and he'd spent three-quarters of an hour listening to Daisy's mother telling him about her rheumatism, and he did have nice wavy fair hair, and . . .

And he was coming round that very evening to have a meat tea with the family. When he accepted Mrs Miller's invitation, there was a kind of a warm meaningfulness in the way he smiled at Daisy that made her heart give a sickly lurch, as if it didn't know whether to go up or down.

So all that afternoon, as she wrapped cakes and sold biscuits and buttered buns in the bakery where she worked, she kept thinking of Dick and sighing, and thinking of Mr Horspath and smiling, and then smiling about Dick and sighing over Mr Horspath, till the silly girl didn't know who she loved and who she didn't. All she knew was that she must be in love with someone, or she wouldn't feel so miserable.

Thunderbolt, meanwhile, was undergoing the most powerful temptation of his life. He was on his way to the Whittles' house for his next trigonometry lesson with another shilling in his pocket, and there outside the Rose and Crown stood Snake-Eyes Melmott himself, talking to a couple of jockey-looking men.

The great bookmaker was a stout prosperous rosy-cheeked man, with a tight check suit, a curly-brimmed bowler hat, and a great gold watch-chain across his middle. He had an air about him of cigars and gold sovereigns, of horses and whisky, of large dinners and boxing-rings.

Thunderbolt slowed down as he went past. Then he stopped. Then he went on more slowly. Then he turned round.

Snake-Eyes Melmott was looking at him benevolently.

'How do, young Thunderbolt,' he said, and his voice was as rich as a plum pudding.

'How do, Mr Melmott,' said Thunderbolt. 'I was just wondering . . .'

'Ah, yes? Anything I can help you with?'

'Er – Dick Smith – you know the business with Daisy, and . . .'

'Mm-hmm.'

'I heard you were offering five to one.'

Snake-Eyes Melmott put his tongue in his cheek, looked around roguishly,

leaned forward, as far as his stomach would let him, and lowered his voice confidentially to say: 'Seeing as you're a good customer, Thunderbolt, and seeing as I've heard from the stable that Mr Horspath's making a very good showing, I can offer you six to one, my boy. Six to one against young Dick.'

Six to one! Thunderbolt glowed. Even the twins hadn't managed to get six to one from the great Snake-Eyes Melmott. It was too tempting to refuse. After all, if he won, he'd be eight shillings to the good, and he could pay for his own trigonometry lessons instead of asking Pa, and he could buy some flowers for Miss Whittle, and . . .

Out came the shilling; out came Snake-Eyes Melmott's little black betting book.

'So you got one bob at two to one, and another bob at sixes. I can see you're a shrewd betting man, young Thunderbolt. I shall have to watch my step with you. Remember the terms of the bet: Dick has got to propose to Daisy, and be accepted, by midnight on the fourteenth. That's two nights away – the night of the Gas-Fitters' Ball.'

Thunderbolt nodded. Snake-Eyes Melmott shook his hand and put away his little black book, and Thunderbolt moved on to the Whittles' house, feeling guilty and excited both at the same time.

And now for the first time he began to take in what Benny had said about Mr Whittle and the pigeon-loft and the stolen silver. He was so excited by the idea of winning more money on Dick that he hadn't remembered that he was going to walk into the house of a desperate criminal.

And as he waited for Miss Honoria Whittle in the dining-room, he realized what it would mean if Mr Whittle was arrested. Unlike Benny, he didn't believe that Miss Whittle was involved at all. Diamond Lou, with a revolver in her stocking! Huh! But that made him feel even guiltier about the shilling bet. That was two shillings he owed her now. She might need those two shillings to live on, if her father was in prison. What would Thunderbolt do if he saw her begging in the street? He'd feel too ashamed for words.

'Hello, Sam,' she said in her friendly way as she came in and sat down with him.

He gulped, and they began their lesson. But he found it hard to concentrate, and kept saying the most unfortunate things.

'Miss Whittle,' he said, 'd'you think your father would let me look after his pigeons, if—'

He stopped suddenly.

'If what, Sam?'

If he goes to prison, was what Thunderbolt had been going to say.

'If . . . if he needs any help,' he finished lamely.

'You could always ask him,' said Miss Whittle. 'Now what about that tangent, Sam? Have another look at it.'

A little later he said, 'Would someone get a longer prison sentence for stealing antique silver than just ordinary silver, Miss?'

'I really don't know,' she said. 'What an odd question. Come on: what's the sine of an angle again? You must try and get it right.'

And finally he said, thinking aloud: 'I suppose Mr Whittle could always escape to Sweden . . .'

'What *are* you talking about?'

'Oh. Sorry, Miss. I was just thinking.'

'Escape, did you say? Escape from what?'

'From a gang,' Thunderbolt made up quickly. 'Of –
er – thieves. Or murderers, even. Seeing as he's been
to Sweden already, he can probably speak Swede, I
expect.'

'Your mind's certainly wandering today, Sam. What
makes you think Papa's been to Sweden?'

'Hasn't he? I thought he went and made a speech
to the European Gas and Coke and Congress and
Manufacturers Council?'

'Oh, that! I see what you mean. No, he was going to
go, but Mr Horspath went instead. Papa thought it
would be a good experience for him.'

'Mr *Horspath*?' Thunderbolt goggled.

'Why, yes. Mr Horspath is the Deputy Manager,
after all. He was very grateful for the opportunity.'

'Did he bring back any matches for Mr Whittle?'

'Matches?'

'Swedish ones. For Mr Whittle's cigars and that.'

'But Papa doesn't smoke. Dear me, Sam, you are
in a curious state this afternoon. What's all this about
matches?'

'Oh! Er – umm – I collect 'em. For my Museum. Different kinds of matches.'

'And why are you so interested in Mr Horspath?'

''Cause – 'cause he's courting Daisy Miller.'

'Ah, I see . . . But what about Dick Smith? The poor man with the phobia? Hasn't he managed to propose yet?'

Thunderbolt tried to collect his wits, and told her about the incident in the Music Hall. She laughed gently.

'Poor man! And Daisy too. A bowl of bananas, you say? Oh dear! No, it's not very tactful, is it.'

He wondered whether to tell her about the secret of love, as revealed by Orlando, but it was time to go; and in any case he was bursting to get back to the hideout, find Benny and the others, and tell them this astonishing news about Mr Horspath.

As for Mr Horspath himself, that elegant and wavy-haired gentleman was knocking on the door of the Millers' house at that very moment, clasping a large bunch of roses and wearing his best light tweed suit, with a purple cravat fastened in the fashionable new style with a little silver ring.

The Millers wanted to make a good impression on Mr Horspath, because he just might want to propose to Daisy, you never knew. Mr Miller had been made to put his best suit on, which made him hot and fidgety, and told to be polite and not pour his tea into the saucer to cool it, which made him cross.

'Blooming fuss,' he grumbled. 'What's the matter with young Dick then? Why d'you want to marry this popinjay?'

'He's not a popinjay, Pa, he's a Deputy Gasworks Manager. And as for Dick, the less said the better,' said Daisy, who couldn't think of anything else to say about him anyway.

When Mr Horspath knocked at the door Mrs Miller was just rushing to the dining-table with a dish of beetroot salad.

'Oh! There he is! Daisy, come here – you got a smudge on your cheek. Albert, cut that ham nice and thin. And don't you *dare* do that silly trick with the cucumber. I shall die. Quick, Daisy! Open the door!'

Mr Horspath came in and shook hands all round, and presented Mrs Miller with the roses, and then they all sat down at the table to eat the substantial meat tea Mrs Miller and Daisy had prepared. There was ham and tongue and tinned salmon, there was beetroot and tomatoes and lettuce and cucumber, there was thin bread and butter, and there was strawberries and cream to follow.

'What a splendid repast!' Mr Horspath said.

'The re-past is all right,' said Mr Miller, 'but what about the re-future, eh?'

'Oh! Ha ha!' said Mr Horspath, showing his appreciation of Mr Miller's wit. 'Jolly good!'

Mr Miller was pleased to have his little joke laughed at, and went on: 'Here, Mr Horspath. Would you say this was a warm evening?'

'Jolly warm, yes. Splendid weather.'

'Now when I was in the Army,' said Mr Miller, 'out in India, we had a little dodge that we used to get up to to keep ourselves cool. What you do is—'

Mr Miller kicked him on one ankle, and Daisy kicked him on another, but he had his best boots on, and they were pinching his toes so tightly that the kicks came as a welcome relief. He ignored them and went on.

'What you do is, you cut a nice long piece of cucumber peel, like this' – he cut one for himself, and handed another to Mr Horspath – 'and you stick it on your forehead. Go on, try.'

He stuck his own on, and Mr Horspath did the same with his. They sat there looking at each other.

'Remarkable cooling properties, cucumber,' said Mr Miller.

'Jolly cool, yes,' said Mr Horspath, nodding. The cucumber peel slid down his nose. He had the uncomfortable feeling that Mr Miller was laughing at him, though the other man was looking inscrutably solemn.

After the meal Mrs Miller said, 'Daisy, dear, do take Mr Horspath into the parlour. Your Pa and me has got things to do in the kitchen.'

The way she looked at her husband made it clear that she was going to tell him off about the cucumber business, but Mr Horspath pretended not to notice that and stood up politely to open the door for Daisy.

'This way, Mr Horspath,' said Daisy, who could have

whacked her father over the head with his wretched cucumber. Every time she brought someone nice home, he had to go and make them stick cucumber peel all over themselves and look silly. She could have cried.

But Mr Horspath was so nice he didn't seem to mind.

'I say, Daisy,' he said when they were sitting on the little sofa, 'I wish you'd call me Bertie.'

'Oh, thank you!' said Daisy, shyly tweaking a frond of the enormous potted palm that stood behind the sofa. This potted palm was Mr Miller's pride and joy. He claimed he had grown it from a coconut that a monkey in India had thrown at him, but no one really believed that. It was so big now that it almost filled the space between the sofa and the window, and darkened the room considerably.

Mr Horspath sat a little closer and slid his arm along the back of the sofa behind Daisy.

'Daisy,' he murmured, 'I'm so glad we're alone at last. I've wanted to be alone with you for weeks and weeks . . .'

And she felt little shivers going all the way up and down her spine, as if mice were dancing on her. She even heard little mouse-like rustlings from somewhere in the room. How embarrassing! She hoped Mr Horspath wouldn't notice.

All this time, the twins had been preparing the way for Dick to unleash the power of Orlando's love secret. Knowing nothing about Mr Horspath's visit to the Millers', they had arranged for Dick to crouch unseen behind the privet hedge in the Millers' little front garden, and then clamber through the front window like a lover in a play. Daisy often sat in the parlour of an evening, and he could make his declaration of love without being interrupted.

So very, very carefully and quietly Angela raised the window and held aside the thick palm-leaves that got in the way.

'Look,' she whispered, 'there's her hand already, on the back of the sofa. All you gotta do is grab it and cover it with burning kisses.'

Dick, trembling with resolution, stepped through with no more noise than a mouse. He could see the hand where Angela was pointing – a soft, delicate, pale hand. It could only be Daisy's. He was nearly there!

'Go *on*,' whispered Zerlina.

Dick nodded, took a deep breath, closed his eyes, and grabbed.

What happened next was never entirely clear to anyone.

First, the potted palm fell over with a mighty crash.

Then Daisy gave a yell of alarm.

Then Mr Horspath stood up in horror and gazed open-mouthed at his own right hand, which was being covered with burning kisses by a blushing Dick, whose eyes were screwed tight shut.

Before anyone could speak, Dick (who'd been counting) came to the twelfth burning kiss and pressed Mr Horspath's hand to his heart.

'I loves yer!' he bawled hoarsely. 'Will yer marry me?'

'WHAT?' shrieked Mr Horspath.

Dick opened his eyes.

His jaw fell.

He looked at Mr Horspath, at Daisy, at the potted palm, at his own hand, still clutching Mr Horspath's.

He let it go as if it was electrified.

'You snake in the grass!' he shouted, and punched Mr Horspath right on the nose.

Angela and Zerlina cheered loudly.

'Go it, Dick!' they cried. 'Whack him again!'

Mr Horspath clutched his nose with a shrill cry, and then events got out of control, as the twins told Benny and Thunderbolt later.

Unknown to anyone, PC Jellicoe had been passing by, and hearing the noise of a disturbance of the peace, he blew his whistle vigorously and lumbered to the scene.

Mr and Mrs Miller heard the noise too, even over their discussion of the cucumber business, and came hurrying in to see what was going on.

They found Mr Horspath trying to mop his nose and hide behind Daisy while Dick chased him furiously, waving his fists.

'Come on out and fight, you wavy-haired weasel!' Dick roared.

'No – no – help!' cried Mr Horspath. 'He's assaulting me! Help!'

'Stop it, Dick! Stop it!' cried Daisy.

'Help! Police!' shouted Mrs Miller. 'Murder!'

'Go on, Dick, clock him another one,' said

Mr Miller, but then he saw the ruins of his potted palm, and struck his forehead in horror. 'My potted palm!' he shouted. 'I grew that meself from a coconut! Who's done that? Was that you, Horsface?'

'No!' sobbed Mr Horspath, dodging behind Daisy again. 'It was him!'

'Come here! Come out and take yer medicine!' bellowed Dick, bouncing up and down and waving his fists. 'Making up to Daisy like that! Blooming sauce! I'll teach yer to—'

But what Dick intended to teach Mr Horspath they never heard, because PC Jellicoe, looking in at the window, blew such a blast on his whistle that they all fell still with their ears ringing.

'Woss going on?' PC Jellicoe demanded. 'Is this a private and domestic dispute, or do you require the assistance of the law?'

'Constable, arrest this man!' blubbered Mr Horspath. 'And as for your position at the gasworks, Smiss, you can consider yourself dismithed!'

'Eh?' said Daisy.

'You can't do that!' said Dick. 'This ain't nothing to

do with the blooming gasworks – this is a matter of love and honour!'

'I can do what I like,' said Mr Horspath, mopping his nose, feeling a bit safer now that PC Jellicoe had clambered in through the window to protect him. 'And you heard what I said. You're sacked!'

With a roar, Dick sprang at him again. He managed to get in one good wallop. Mr Horspath went down with a shriek, and then PC Jellicoe got the handcuffs on Dick, who was struggling like an eel.

Outside the window, in the shadow of the privet hedge, the twins looked at each other. They didn't need to speak. Leaving the confusion of wailing and shouting and banging behind them, they softly and suddenly vanished away.

'So he's arrested,' said Angela.

'In *gaol*?' said Benny.

'Yeah!' said Zerlina. 'We watched old Jelly belly drag him away in handcuffs. Half the street was watching!'

'So . . .' Thunderbolt gulped. 'If he's in gaol . . . He

can't ask Daisy to ... And the Gas-Fitters' Ball's the day after tomorrow ...'

'Did you put that other shilling on with Snake-Eyes?' said Angela.

He nodded speechlessly.

'Cor,' said Zerlina.

They looked at him with pity and wonder, as if he were a ruined man already. Thunderbolt felt the shadow of the workhouse looming over him – and worse. He was thinking of the melodrama he and Pa had been to see the week before called 'The Primrose Path, or If Only He Had Known', in which a fine young man descended step by easy step along the road to ruin. Drink; low companions; loose women, whatever they were; and – Thunderbolt gulped – it had all started with gambling. The young man in the play had begun by betting the rent money on a horse-race and ended up on the gallows, and the last scene of all showed his poor mother weeping in the snow outside the prison walls as the bell tolled eight o'clock, the execution hour.

Thunderbolt opened his mouth once or twice, but

couldn't speak. Suddenly that felt like his future, too.

'Right,' said Benny. 'We gotta do summing about this. You two gotta get Dick out of gaol, 'cause you got him in. Oh yes you blooming did,' he went on hotly as the twins started to argue. 'Never mind blooming Snake-Eyes Melmott and five to one and winning fortunes and so on. Dick's in gaol and he didn't oughter be and you gotta get him out. I don't care what you do – you make sure he's there at the Gas-Fitters' Ball. Meanwhile, me and Thunderbolt's got summing even more difficult and dangerous to do. We might end up in gaol ourselves for it, but it's gotta be done. It wouldn't be right otherwise. So there,' he finished, glaring around pugnaciously. 'Anyone arguing? Good. Now let's get on with it!'

Five

The Ladder

The twins weren't allowed to know what Benny and Thunderbolt were doing, in case they were caught and tortured. If they didn't know, they couldn't confess.

'Like Garibaldi and the Redshirts,' said Angela, 'fighting the Austrians.'

There was an engraved portrait of the great Italian hero above the sideboard in their parlour. They'd never been entirely clear about what he'd done, but they were sure it was very gallant and dangerous.

As their task was now. They walked home slowly, talking under their breath, leaning together slightly in the curious way they did when they were plotting something. More than one person who saw them crossed their fingers superstitiously, having seen them in action before.

At supper they hardly noticed what they were eating. Their mother had to bang the table and reach meaningfully for the breadknife before they came out of their mutual trance.

'What's up, gals?' said their father, a cheerful soul.

'Nothing,' said Angela.

'They're in trouble,' said their brother Alf. 'I can tell.'

'No we ain't,' said Zerlina.

'Well, if they're not yet, they're gonna be,' said their other brother Giuseppe, or Joe for short. Like their father, he worked in the dried-fruit trade.

'They get in a trouble, I cut a their troats,' said their mother, feeling the edge of the breadknife. Most of the Peretti men had been born in London, which was why they spoke better English than Italian, and they used to go back to Naples to find a wife, which was why their wives spoke better Italian than English.

'I should cut 'em anyway,' suggested Giuseppe.

'Save time. Here, Alf, fancy a stroll down the Walk later on? We might have a drink with Orlando.'

The twins felt a little shiver of excitement, and, because they were twins, each of them knew that the other had felt it at the same moment. The same cat-like smile appeared on their faces, and they turned their attention to the lasagne.

Much later, when darkness had fallen over Lambeth, when the hissing naphtha-lamps of the market stalls had all been put away, when only the grimy moonlight glimmered on the rough bricks and the dirty cobbles, two small figures trudged along beside the great grim wall of the prison.

Their heads were bowed; each of them held a big white handkerchief to her face; occasionally a sniff or even a broken sob would make its way out.

Just as they reached the little iron-studded oak door that was set into a big and even more iron-studded oak gate, a key turned, and the door creaked open. It was midnight: the hour when the prison warders changed shifts.

The little figures looked up tragically at the first man who came out. He was a big, ponderous man with a grey moustache; and when he saw the two girls gazing up at him imploringly, with the moonlight glittering on the tears on their cheeks, he couldn't help stopping.

'What's the matter?' he said.

'It's our brother,' said Angela.

'He in here, is he?'

Angela gave a little sob and hid her face in the handkerchief. The warder shifted his feet uncomfortably, for he too had been to see 'The Primrose Path', and had found it as moving as Thunderbolt did.

'He's ... He's not a bad man,' said Zerlina piteously, 'but he's passionate and impetuous.'

'And now we're all alone,' said Angela.

'We just want to know where he is,' said Zerlina, 'so we can wave to him and ... and ...'

'And pray for him,' Angela put in quickly.

'That's it, yeah,' said Zerlina. 'If only we knew which cell he was in we could feel a bit easier in our minds.'

''Cause we could come and just look up and ... and think about him,' said Angela brokenly.

The warder felt a lump in his throat. He coughed hard.

'What's his name?' he said as sternly as he could manage.

'Dick Smith,' said Zerlina. 'He's not a *bad* man. He *means* good.'

'Ah, yes, Smith,' said the warder. 'Number 1045. He's in the East Wing. That's round here. You follow me, gals, and I'll show yer.'

He led them round the corner of the great grim wall and pointed to a tiny window high up under the edge of the roof.

'That's his cell, the third on the left,' he said. 'You could wave to him from here.'

'Oh, thank you, sir, thank you!' said Angela.

'You're a kind and noble man!' said Zerlina.

The warder brushed a manly tear from his eye. What a pair of angels!

'Well, I must say,' he said, 'he's a lucky feller to have such devoted sisters. I shouldn't wonder but what your love and devotion wouldn't make all the difference to a young lad like him. A good example like that might set him on the road to reform.' He began to walk off, and turned back to say, 'Who knows? With your help, he might not be in here for long'.

Oddly enough, that was exactly what the twins had in mind.

Their next stop was Charlie Ladysmith's builder's yard, next to the Candle Manufactory. It was locked, of course, in the middle of the night, but there was a loose panel in the wooden fence, and it only took a moment for the girls to slip through.

'You know what?' whispered Angela. 'They oughter make things like this for cats to come in through doors with.'

'No one'd buy 'em,' said Zerlina. 'It's a silly idea.'

'Yeah, perhaps it is. Now where's he keep them ladders?'

Charlie Ladysmith wasn't a very tidy builder, or he'd have repaired his fence by this time, but it didn't take long to find his ladders. They were leaning against the wall of the main shed, long ones, short ones, stepladders and platform ladders.

'Cor,' whispered Angela. 'They're blooming long, all of 'em. Even the short ones is long.'

'How we gonna get one of them out?' said Zerlina.

It turned out to be easier than they'd thought. They only knocked over a pile of bricks, smashed a window, tipped a rain-water barrel over onto a heap of sand, jabbed a hole in the wall of the shed, and broke two more panels on the fence; and after twenty minutes' struggling, they had the longest ladder they could manage outside in the street.

'He better preciate this,' said Zerlina, panting. 'He better be grateful.'

Angela's eyes glittered with the thought of what they'd do to Dick if he didn't and wasn't. But they didn't have time to think about that; they had another call to make that night.

Being in the theatrical profession, the Mighty Orlando was used to staying in boarding-houses. There were good ones and bad ones. When he was working in London, he always stayed at Mrs Drummond's in Tower Street, where the landlady looked after him well, providing two loaves, three dozen eggs and five pounds of bacon for breakfast every day, as well as an extra strong bed to sleep in and a nice quiet room

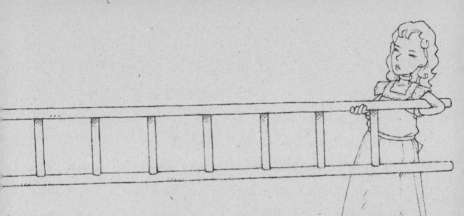

overlooking the back yard.

It was half-past one in the morning when the twins clambered over the wall into that very back yard, and looked up at the house, wondering which window was Orlando's.

It wasn't hard to tell, actually. Since it was a warm night, all the windows were open, and out of one of them came a snoring so thunderous that the twins were lost in admiration.

'Like an elephant!' said Angela.

'Or a railway engine. It's colossal!'

'How we gonna wake him up? Whatever noise we make, he won't hear it 'cause of the noise he's making hisself!'

In the end they threw stones through the window. Orlando was used to cannon-balls landing on his head, of course, so he hardly noticed a few pebbles; but finally, by luck, one of them landed in his open mouth. He swallowed it like a fly and woke up.

The twins heard the snoring stop with a sort of gulping noise. A moment or two later, Orlando appeared at the window, with a big white night-cap keeping the draughts off his shiny head.

'Who's that?' he said, peering down. 'Oh, it's you, gals. What can I do for yer?'

'Rescue someone from prison,' said Angela.

'It's easy,' said Zerlina. 'It'll only take ten minutes, honest.'

'Only if he's been unjustly accused,' said Orlando sternly. 'I takes a dim view of any hanky-panky with the law.'

'It's Dick,' said Angela. 'You remember that love secret you told him?'

'Yeah. How'd he get on?'

'He kissed the wrong hand and proposed to Mr Horspath by mistake,' said Zerlina, 'and they put him in gaol.'

Orlando was appalled.

'That's a monstrous piece of injustice!' he said, struggling into his clothes. 'I never heard the like! And it's my fault, and all. I oughter told him the first part of the love secret.'

'What's that?'

'Make sure you got hold of the proper hand. It's an easy mistake to make, especially when you're flustered. I spect Dick was a bit flustered. That's probly how it happened.'

They were all speaking in whispers, not wanting to wake the other lodgers. Orlando tiptoed downstairs and out of the kitchen door, and a few moments later they were on their way to prison. The twins told him more about the potted palm and Dick's unfortunate accident.

Orlando shook his head in dismay.

'I knew a trapeze artist once as made a similar mistake,' he said. 'Course, grabbing hold of the wrong hand in that profession is the last thing you want to do. Matter of fact, I think it was the last thing he *did* do. Where's this prison, then?'

They reached the prison, and the twins retrieved the

ladder from the alley nearby where they'd left it.

'It's that window at the end,' whispered Angela.

'All right,' said Orlando. 'Now you two better keep watch in case a copper comes along. I shouldn't wonder but what he might think it was a bit suspicious.'

And he propped the ladder against the wall and began to climb up.

Dick was lying on his bunk dreaming of Daisy and Mr Horspath. She was telling him to put slices of cucumber on his black eye, and he was saying, 'Daisy, your face is like the moon rising over the gasworks! Marry me at once!'

Dick growled in his sleep. Couldn't he even have a dream without that silky-handed stoat turning up in it?

So he was pleased to hear a knocking at the bars of his cell, and to wake up and see a broad-shouldered figure outlined against the dark sky.

'Psst!' came a mighty whisper. 'Dick!'

'Who's that? That's not Orlando, is it? What you doing here?'

'I come to rescue yer,' said Orlando. 'You better

stand back. I can't answer for the strength of these walls.'

And he took hold of the bars and pulled them apart as if they were made of pastry. There was a great wrenching noise, and bricks and bits of stone fell down.

'Cor,' breathed Dick. 'Blimey!'

'Out yer come, then,' said Orlando.

'Can I come too?' said a shaky voice from the lower bunk, and a furtive-looking little man peered out, blinking and scratching his head.

'Who's that?' said Orlando, peering in.

'That's Sid the Swede,' said Dick. 'We turned out to be sharing a cell.'

'Oh, go on,' said Sid the Swede. 'Be a sport.'

He sat up and clasped his hands pleadingly.

'What you in here for?' said Orlando sternly. 'I ain't letting dangerous criminals out, only honest men what's been wrongly convicted.'

'I stole a couple of pillow-cases off a washing-line,' said Sid the Swede.

'What for?'

But before Sid the Swede could answer that, a

bell began to ring loudly, and pounding feet were heard running along the corridors towards the cell.

'That's the alarm!' said Dick. 'They must've heard you tearing the bars out, Orlando!'

'No time to waste, then,' said Orlando. 'You come down the ladder first, Dick, and then I'll let this gentleman out, being as he seems harmless enough. But mind,' he said, wagging a massive finger at Sid the Swede, 'any further law-breaking, and I shall be sorely disappointed in you. I couldn't answer for my temper in that case.'

'Yes! Yes! Anything!' squeaked Sid the Swede. 'I promise!'

So Orlando moved down the ladder, and

Dick clambered out after him, and finally, hopping and squirming and yelping with fear, Sid the Swede came too.

'Quick! Quick!' the twins were calling, for a policeman's whistle was blowing from the very next street.

Orlando and the two escaped convicts got to the bottom and scampered away after the two girls, not pausing for breath till they were safely back near the New Cut Gang's hideout over the stable. There they stopped, panting and triumphant.

'We never took Charlie Ladysmith's ladder back,' said Angela.

'Never mind,' said Zerlina, 'he'll be famous. Folks'll buy him drinks for days on account of having his ladder nicked for the great break-out.'

'But what am I going to do, gals?' said Dick. 'I mean, I'm glad to be out, and all, but I can't live the life of a fugitive. I'm a law-abiding bloke.'

'Yeah, so am I,' said Sid the Swede eagerly. 'I never been in trouble in me life. I shall have to clear me name, else I shan't be able to hold me head up.'

'And how are you gonna do that?' said Orlando.

'I shall just have to tell the truth about the pillow-case business,' said Sid the Swede. 'No matter what the cost to my dignity. I value my reputation for truth and honesty. Well, goodnight all. And thank you, Mr – Whatever. You're a gentleman.'

He held out his hand to Orlando, who shook his head.

'No, no,' he said, 'better not. Find a rock and I'll show yer why.'

'Another time, perhaps, eh?' said Sid the Swede, and scuttled away.

'You better stay in the hideout tonight, Dick,' said Angela. 'We'll bring you some breakfast in the morning.'

'You only got to keep out the way till tomorrow night, anyway,' said Zerlina.

'Why?'

''Cause it's the Gas-Fitters' Ball tomorrow, and you're going,' said Angela. 'Everyone's gotta be there. And you can go in costume if you like, with a mask.'

Dick's mouth opened and closed, but no words came out of it.

'Anyway,' said Zerlina, 'we got another plan, ain't we, Ange?'

'Oh, yeah,' said Angela. 'We thought of it when you was up the ladder arguing. It's the best one yet. You'll be amazed, I promise.'

'Now get in quick, and stay clear of Jasper. He's bad-tempered at both ends.'

'All right,' said Dick meekly. 'I dunno what it is about you gals, I just can't argue with yer. Can you, Orlando?'

'I never could argue with a lady,' said the strong man, watching the girls run off into the dark as quick as sparks up a chimney. 'Well, good night, Dick. I'll see you at the ball.'

Six

The Lambeth Bandit

All over Lambeth, people were getting ready for the Gas-Fitters' Ball.

The musicians of the Prince of Wales's Own Light Bombardiers, who were going to play for the dancing, were polishing their trombones and tightening their drums; the caterers were making ice-creams and soups and custards and pies and sandwiches of every sort; dressmakers were tightening straps and loosen-ing waistbands and hemming edges and sewing on lace.

And the detectives from Scotland Yard, under the direction of Inspector Gorman, were making no progress at all with the case of the Gas-Fitters' Hall silver.

'All the usual villains seem to be on holiday, Inspector,' said the sergeant.

'Well, try the unusual ones,' said the inspector crossly. 'Try everyone.'

'What about Sid the Swede and this prison break-out last night?'

'Yes,' said the inspector, scratching his chin. 'Sid couldn't have nicked the silver, but it's a curious business. The other bloke who got out was some young gas-fitter convicted of assault and battery . . .' Then he realized what he'd said. 'A gas-fitter!'

The two policemen looked at each other, wide-eyed.

'You don't think *he* could have been involved in the burglary?' said the sergeant.

'Well, it's highly suspicious, to say the least. When he turns up, we better pull him in for questioning.'

'D'you think he will turn up, Inspector?'

'Of course! Scotland Yard always gets its man. There's dozens of trained sleuths looking for him right now, not to mention bloodhounds. He won't be free for long. And when he's put away next time, it'll be for a good long stretch.'

At the very moment, Dick was sitting in the gang's hideout chewing a stale currant bun and washing it down with a bottle of cold tea, and trying not to think about policemen. The twins had brought the food to him early that morning, and they were now basking in Benny's praise.

'You done all right,' he said, 'and no error. That must've took some doing, organizing a jail-break. Course me and Thunderbolt could've done it ourselves, only we had summing even harder to do.'

'What was that then?' said Angela.

'I better not tell you yet,' said Benny, 'on account of being caught and tortured. You'll find out tonight. But it was desperate and dangerous. And daring. I don't suppose anyone's been as daring as what Thunderbolt and me was last night.'

'Yes, they have,' said Zerlina. 'Me and Ange was. We fooled a prison warder into revealing where Dick was locked up—'

'And we borrowed a ladder from a builder's yard under the nose of a powerful bulldog with jaws *that* big—' said Angela.

'What we had to tame and master with special Italian dog-commands as made it roll over and keep quiet—'

'And we smuggled Orlando out his boarding-house wrapped in a roll of carpet—'

'And we fought off three policemen what tried to capture the ladder Dick was coming down—'

'Did you really?' said Thunderbolt, deeply impressed. 'Cor.'

'Yeah, all right, all right,' said Benny impatiently. 'We *all* been daring and desperate.'

'Yeah,' said Dick, swallowing the last of the currant bun. 'I reckon you have, kids. But I'm wondering what I ought to do next, 'cause I'm on the run now, ain't I? I'm a wanted man. There's probly a price on me head.'

'Better be a big 'un,' said Angela, 'the trouble we went through. They better not offer just half a crown.'

'In Sicily,' said Zerlina, 'when someone breaks out of jail, they go up in the hills and join the bandits and live in a cave.'

'Not many hills in Lambeth,' said Dick. 'Nor caves neither. I dunno if Daisy'd want to live in a cave, somehow.'

'She would if you asked her,' said Angela.

'Course she would,' said Zerlina. ''Cause she'd listen to you with a lot more respect if you was a bandit. She'd have to. Else you'd shoot her.'

'Or cut her froat,' said Angela.

'Well—' began Dick.

'And you'd be able to ask her, too! You know the reason you couldn't ask her before?' said Zerlina.

'Yeah. I was too blooming shy,' said Dick.

'No! The *real* reason was, you was a gas-fitter. If you was a bandit, you wouldn't be nervous of nothing. You'd be bold and daring.'

'Would I?'

'Course you would,' said Angela.

And it was true, too. Dick felt himself become braver, more desperate, more daring, just by thinking about it. Dick Smith, a Wanted Man! Dangerous Dick Smith, the Lambeth Bandit!

'Yeah,' he said. 'I reckon you're right. I could do

anything now! If Daisy was here I'd — I'd propose to her on the spot. No error!'

'Well, wait till tonight,' said Benny, ''cause you can do it at the ball. You gotta be in disguise, of course. With a mask. And what *we* gotta do,' he said to the rest of the gang, 'is we gotta be there and all. We can work in the kitchens or summing. 'Cause everything's gonna happen tonight. The Gas-Fitters' Hall burglar's gonna be revealed!'

'And Dick's going to win his bet!' said Thunderbolt.

'Eh? What bet?' said Dick.

There was an awkward silence. Everyone looked at Thunderbolt, who suddenly realized what he'd said, and corrected himself quickly.

'I mean, propose to Daisy,' he said. 'I didn't mean bet at all. I was thinking of something quite different. I didn't mean Dick had made a bet on it. I mean, I didn't mean *anyone* had made a bet on it. I mean, proposed to Daisy. I mean—'

'Oh, stow it,' said Benny, 'we got no time for riddles. We gotta go and see the caterer and get ourselves jobs. You keep out of sight, Dick, remember, you're on the run. You can't slip out and have half a pint down the Feathers. If you get thirsty you'll have to wait till we bring you another bottle of tea or summing. And yer costume for later. I tell yer, mates, this is the best plan I ever had! This is a stunner!'

'And we got a plan and all,' said Zerlina smugly. 'Ain't we, Ange?'

But they refused to say what it was, in case of torture.

Daisy didn't know whether to feel sorrier for Dick, or for Mr Horspath with his spectacular black eye, or herself. In the end she felt sorry for all three of them in turn.

Another thing she didn't know was whether or not to go to the ball. Mr Horspath had asked her, but she thought that Dick *would* have asked her if he'd got round to it, and she'd rather go with him; on the other hand, Dick was in gaol and Mr Horspath wasn't, and Mr Horspath had brought her a huge bunch of lilies only that morning and asked her again to go with him; and altogether the poor girl was scarcely in her right mind.

'I just dunno what to do, Ma!' she said after work.

'There, there, dear,' said Mrs Miller. 'If I was you I'd go with that nice Mr Horspath. He's a real gentleman.'

'I wouldn't if *I* was her,' said Mr Miller darkly. 'I don't think she'd be safe in his hands. A man what can treat a potted palm in that shocking and cold-blooded way is capable of any villainy.'

So Daisy dithered, and she might have gone on dithering for ever if Angela hadn't called, late in the afternoon, with a message for her ears only.

'I can't stop long,' said Angela breathlessly when they were in the parlour, 'but I came to say you gotta go to the ball, 'cause Dick's going to be there in disguise. He escaped from prison specially. Not even prison walls could keep him away from you. Not even crocodiles or machine-guns either, probly. And anyway you gotta be there for – for a special other reason. I gotta go now, but you *better* be there, or else.'

'Yes! Right! I will!' said Daisy. She was thrilled.

Angela scampered off, and Daisy shot upstairs to put on her ball dress.

* * *

And in every household in Lambeth, almost, people were putting on their finery. Some were going in fancy dress, and some weren't, because you could choose which you liked. Most of the younger people were going in costume, but the more respectable ones went in ordinary evening dress.

Mr Horspath, as a Deputy Gasworks Manager,

thought he'd better be respectable, so he put on a white tie and black tail-coat, and anointed his hair with Bandoline to keep it in place and maintain the waviness people found so attractive. He had wondered what to do about his black eye until he found an advertisement in the *Gentlemen's Gazette*, and hurried along at once to Mr George Paul, of Oxford Street, an Artist in Black Eye.

Mr Paul covered the wounded organ with theatrical make-up, and charged Mr Horspath half a crown for it; and now, as he peered into the mirror, it looked almost normal again. Daisy would be tremendously impressed, he thought, and he practised a specially charming smile two or three times till he got it right.

The Kaminskys were all going, too. Mr Kaminsky and Cousin Morris had spent hours arguing about whether or not the latest style in evening wear, the 'dress lounge', was suitable for such a high-toned affair as the Gas-Fitters' Ball.

'A tailor's got to innovate, Louis!' said Cousin Morris. 'He's got to be at the forefront of fashion!'

'No, no, no,' said Mr Kaminsky. 'A tailor's got to reflect the quiet good taste of traditional opinion. It's no good flaunting all your latest American fashions, not in Lambeth, anyway. You wear that dress lounge if you want to; I'm sticking to formal evening wear. Look at the cut of this waistcoat, now! Look at the shine on that lapel, eh! A thing of beauty is a joy for ever, Morris.'

In the Dobney household, Thunderbolt's Pa was ironing his best trousers. Thunderbolt had wanted his father to go as a pirate, but Pa said he'd only worn this suit three times and hardly got his money's worth out of it; so he fetched it out of the wardrobe and set the iron on the stove and got to work. A pungent smell of moth-balls was filling the little kitchen. Or *was* it mothballs?

Mr Dobney sniffed.

'Can you smell burning, Sam?' he said.

'Cor, yeah!' said Thunderbolt in alarm. 'You got the iron too hot, Pa! Take it off quick!'

Mr Dobney snatched the iron off his trousers just in time, and scratched his head.

'I dunno what it is, I can't seem to get it right. Your Ma never used to have any trouble with it.'

'What Mrs Malone does,' said Thunderbolt, 'she puts a wet cloth on it and irons through that. It goes all steamy.'

'Ah,' said Mr Dobney. 'I knew there was a secret to it.'

He put the iron back on the range to keep hot and dipped his handkerchief in the dishwater. This time the iron hissed and steamed properly, and beautiful sharp creases appeared down the trouser-legs.

'Smashing,' said Mr Dobney admiringly. 'You could slice a cucumber with them creases.'

The Peretti brothers, meanwhile, were criticizing each other's costumes. Alf was going as a gondolier, but he had so many rings in his ears and fake jewellery all over him that Giuseppe said he looked more like a chandelier.

'No, no, you got to be a bit showy,' said Alf. 'Make the best of yerself. The young ladies like a bit of show. I can't see 'em being impressed by them great caterpillars on your legs.'

Giuseppe was going as a cowboy, with a ten-gallon hat he could only just get through the door and huge furry chaps over his trousers.

'No, this is the tough and manly look,' he said. 'If it's good enough for Buffalo Bill, it's good enough for me.'

Alf twiddled his moustache and smirked.

And finally, in the Whittle household, Miss Honoria was pinning a gardenia to her ball gown. The flower had arrived by special messenger, with a card that said 'From an unknown admirer', and she hoped that if she wore it to the ball, she might find out who had sent it.

'Very pretty, my dear,' said Mr Whittle. 'It's a shame you've only got your old father to go to the ball with.'

'Not at all, Papa, you look very handsome,' said Miss Whittle, kissing his cheek and adjusting his bow tie.

So everyone was ready for the ball.

'What's this plan of yours, then?' said Benny to the twins, as they hurried towards the kitchen entrance of Gas-Fitters' Hall.

'Ah ha,' said Angela. 'It's the best one yet.'

'You remember the Archbishop of Canterbury stunt?' said Zerlina.

'What, when you got the Archbishop to come and judge the cat show? That was a laugh, that was. Is he coming to the ball, then?'

'No,' said Angela.

'Well, who is?' said Thunderbolt, bewildered.

'Ah ha,' said Zerlina. 'You wait and see.'

'You never got anyone!' said Benny.

'Betcher,' said the twins together.

The boys looked at each other. Never bet against the twins, was Benny's rule through life.

'H'mm,' was all he could find to say.

'Yes,' said Angela contentedly as they moved on. 'I bet you never had such a surprise as what we arranged tonight.'

'Oh, yeah? Well, I bet our surprise is better'n yours,' retorted Benny, forgetting his lifelong rule at once.

However, there was no time to think of surprises once the work began. Benny and Thunderbolt were going to be pageboys, and the twins were going to help in the cloakroom, so they'd all be able to keep an eye on what was going on.

Gas-Fitters' Hall had been decorated in grand style. The ballroom was festooned with flowers and ribbons; dainty little tables and chairs were set along the sides, and a table as long as a cricket pitch was covered in a snowy white cloth on which stood piles of gleaming plates, lines of sparkling glasses, and boxes of silver cutlery for the buffet supper later on. On the bandstand, the musicians of the Prince of Wales's Own

Light Bombardiers were taking their places, under the direction of their conductor, Lieutenant-Colonel Fidler. The dancing floor had been polished till it shone like silk.

In the kitchen, squads of cooks and under-cooks were putting the final touches to the salmon in aspic, the veal-and-ham pies, the Madeira trifles. The wine waiters were polishing their corkscrews, the ordinary waiters were smoothing down the white napkins over their left forearms, and the head waiter was calculating how much he was likely to get in tips. Everything was ready.

The first guests began to arrive soon after eight o'clock. The twins were interested to see how many of them had come in evening dress, and how many in costume. Four Demon Kings arrived in the first ten minutes, and four Gypsy Maidens, and they all stood round awkwardly trying not to look at each other until more people arrived.

'There's Alf and Giuseppe, look!' said Angela, as their big brothers came swaggering in. 'And who's that in the Arab Chieftain get-up?'

A figure dressed in white robes from head to foot was shuffling into the ballroom. The robes were a bit too big for him, or he was a bit too small for them, and he tripped and fell full length.

'He's going to make a big impression,' said Zerlina. 'On the floor, anyway.'

'Here, look! Mr Horspath!'

Mr Horspath came in smiling widely, ran a careless hand over his hair to check that the waves were all still in place, and handed his top hat and gloves to Zerlina.

'Here you are, my girl,' he said. 'Look after them well, and there might be a sixpence for you.'

And he went into the ballroom, smiling at everyone in sight.

'I thought he was going with Daisy?' said Angela.

'Here's Daisy now, with her Pa and Ma,' said Zerlina.

When they'd checked in their hats, Mr Miller leaned over confidentially and asked Angela, 'D'you happen to know if they're serving salad with the refreshments?'

'Yeah,' she said. 'Full of cucumbers.'

'Good, good,' he said happily, and strolled into the ballroom.

While Mrs Miller went to attend to her hair, Zerlina told Daisy about Dick.

'He's coming as a bandit,' she said, 'with a black mask on. He's not here yet. I'll tell you as soon as he arrives.'

Daisy was looking very pretty indeed. In fact she was the prettiest young lady there by a long way, and as soon as he saw her, Mr Horspath immediately left the other young lady he'd been talking to and made straight for Daisy as if he was on rails.

'Miss Miller! Daisy!' he said. 'I'm so glad you could come! Do let me have the first dance.'

'Well,' she said, 'I dunno really.'

'But the musicians are striking up! The night is young! And how beautiful you look in your— Yes? What is it?'

There was a small, untidy pageboy plucking at his sleeve.

'Sandwich, guvnor?' said the pageboy, holding up a

plate of them and shoving up some remarkably dirty spectacles.

'Oh, yes, yes, all right – have a sandwich, my dear,' he said to Daisy.

Daisy took a sandwich and began to nibble it very daintily.

'What about you?' said the pageboy to Mr Horspath. 'Don't you want one?'

'Oh, all right,' said Mr Horspath, to get rid of him. But the boy stayed there, glaring at him fixedly. Mr Horspath began to get nervous.

'Go away,' he said 'Shoo. Go and feed someone else.'

The boy drifted away, but he didn't take his eyes off Mr Horspath for a moment.

'Ha ha,' said Mr Horspath to Daisy. 'Amusing little rascal.'

'I thought he was sweet,' said Daisy. 'He looked like young Thunderbolt from Clayton Terrace.'

'Daisy,' Mr Horspath murmured, moving a little closer to her, 'I'm glad we're alone. I want to ask you— Yes? Yes? What do you want?'

For another pageboy had appeared, with a plate of sausage rolls. This boy was bigger than the first one, but he was glaring just as intently.

'Sausage roll?' he said, in the same tone of voice as if he'd said, 'D'you want a fight?'

'No, I don't want a sausage roll,' said Mr Horspath irritably. 'Go away.'

'Well, *she* might,' said the boy, and thrust the plate at Daisy.

'Hello, Benny,' she said. 'Fancy seeing you here. Is your Ma and Pa coming?'

'Yeah,' he said. 'Only not in costume. Leah is, though. She's coming as the Queen of Sheba.'

'Oh, lovely! I wish I'd come in costume now. I could have been a Gypsy Maiden.'

'You look very lovely as you are,' said Mr Horspath gallantly, trying to get between Benny and Daisy. 'Go away, boy. When we want a sausage roll, we'll ask for it.'

Benny glared at him through narrowed eyes, and retreated. Mr Horspath turned back to Daisy.

'Daisy,' he murmured softly. 'May I have the next dance? To waltz around the floor with you in my arms would be— Yes? Yes? Yes? What is it *this* time?'

'I thought you might have finished your sandwich,' said Thunderbolt. 'I got plenty more here.'

'Go away! Go away!'

'There's cucumber in them triangular ones, and the other ones is a sort of fishpaste, I think. I just opened one up to have a look.'

'We don't want—'

'They don't smell of anything in pertickler. I smelled 'em too. I suppose it could be jam.'

This boy was driving him to the point of madness, Mr Horspath felt. And then he looked up and saw Daisy waltzing away with a gondolier.

'*Hnnhmhnnhmmm,*' was the way Thunderbolt would have spelled the sound that came from between Mr Horspath's gritted teeth. Thunderbolt thought it best to move away.

Meanwhile, out by the cloakroom, Angela and Zerlina were talking to Dick, who had just arrived.

He was looking as bandit-like as the New Cut Gang could make him. He wore a black cloak made out of a curtain, two wide leather belts over his shoulders and across his chest for bandoliers, and knee-length riding boots they'd borrowed from the stable. Most of his face was hidden behind a black mask across his eyes and a ferocious black beard made of horsehair and dyed with ink.

'I'm not very comfortable in this get-up,' he whispered to Angela. 'The blooming mask keeps getting in me way. You ain't cut the holes big enough. And the beard's awful scratchy, and these boots is crippling me. Is Daisy here yet?'

'Yeah,' said Zerlina. 'She's dancing with Alf.'

'Oh, Alf, eh?' said Dick, his eyes glittering dangerously behind the mask.

'You don't want to worry about him,' said Angela. 'It's old Horspath what's the real danger. Here, go on, hurry up and get in the ballroom – we got more guests coming in.'

They shoved Dick through the door and into the ballroom, which was now getting crowded. The Major-Domo at the door, who was announcing all the guests as they arrived, asked him for his name.

Dick blinked in alarm, and had to shove the mask back into position.

'Oh – er – my name – yeah – er – Mr Scampolati,' he said hastily. 'From Sicily.'

'Mr Scampolati,' said the Major-Domo loudly. 'From Sicily.'

No one took any notice, so Dick moved into the big room and looked around. As well as Alf the gondolier and Giuseppe the cow-puncher there were eight Demon Kings, three Mad Monks, four Pirates, one Henry the Eighth, one Arab Chieftain, and at least half a dozen men dressed as policemen. Dick found himself standing next to one of them in a crowded corner between dances, and nodded in a friendly way. The policeman nodded back.

'Nice costume, mate,' said Dick.

'This ain't a costume,' said the policeman. 'I'm on duty.'

Dick uttered a strangled whinny.

'You all right?' said the policeman.

'Yeah. I must of swallowed a fly,' mumbled Dick. 'You – er – chasing anyone, then?'

'In a manner of speaking,' said the policeman mysteriously. 'We got word as how the perpetrator of the Gas-Fitters' Hall burglary is likely to be here tonight to make a daring raid on all the ladies' jewels.'

'No, really?'

'Yeah. Seems like it's that feller as broke out of prison last night. A desperate character, by all accounts.'

Dick was speechless.

'Keep your eyes open, eh?' said the policeman, and tapped his nose significantly before moving away.

Blimey, thought Dick, this is awful. The place is crawling with rozzers! He looked around and seemed to see them everywhere, like beetles.

So when he felt a soft hand on his arm he jumped a foot and let out a yelp of fear.

'Dick!' said Daisy. 'It's only me.'

'Heck,' he muttered. 'Daisy! Blimey. Lawks! Come behind this aspidistra . . .'

He led her behind the nearest plant, and from the dark green shadow of the leaves he peered out at the brightly lit dance-floor, where couples were twirling about to the music of 'The Gasworks Polka'.

'Dick!' she said. 'What's the matter?'

'I'm on the run, Daisy!' he said. 'I'm a wanted man. The place is full of coppers all looking for me.'

'I know!' she said, and her eyes glowed with admiration. 'It's ever so daring of you. I think you're wonderful, Dick!'

'Do you?' he said. 'Cor. The thing is, they think I done the burglary.'

'They never!'

'They do. I was just talking to one of 'em. If they catch me, I could get ten years, easy. Probably twenty. Here, d'you like my costume, Daisy?'

'Not half,' she said. 'It suits you marvellous. You look ever so handsome! I can't hardly see your face at all.'

Dick wondered if this was the right moment to propose, but before he could clear his throat and blush and shuffle his feet and begin, there was a rustle, and the leaves of the aspidistra parted.

'Ah, there you are, Daisy!' said the smooth voice of Mr Horspath. 'Naughty, naughty girl! Hiding away from me! Come and dance. You know you promised!'

Dick growled, and Mr Horspath wagged a finger at him.

'Come, come!' he said. 'You mustn't hide the loveliest girl at the ball away like this! Give the other fellows a chance, ha ha!'

Dick frowned as fiercely as he could, but unluckily

this displaced the mask, and he found he couldn't see anything at all. Without thinking he put up his hand to adjust it.

Mr Horspath gasped.

'Wait a minute!' he said, and struck an attitude of horror. 'I know that face! That's Smith, isn't it? You're the scoundrel that— Help! Police! Help! Over here!'

In a fury, Dick tore off his scratchy beard and aimed a punch at Mr Horspath's nose. But it didn't connect, because a burly constable seized his arm. In a second whistles were blowing, heavy boots were thundering across the dance-floor, and Dangerous Dick Smith, the Lambeth Bandit, was firmly in the hands of the law.

'Is this him, Inspector?' said the sergeant.

The music had stopped; all the dancers had spread out in a ring around the group by the aspidistra – Mr Horspath pointing dramatically, Daisy with her hands to her cheeks in despair, and two great big policemen holding a struggling, snarling Dick.

The inspector stepped up and took off Dick's mask.

'Yes,' he said. 'This is him. This is our man. Well done, Mr Horspath, sir!'

And close to the bandstand, Benny and Thunderbolt looked at each other in dismay. This wasn't what they'd planned at all.

But the twins hadn't been fooling when they spoke about a big surprise. Having bagged the Archbishop of Canterbury before, they'd got ambitious, and gone for even bigger game this time – and got it. For suddenly there came a bang on the floor from the Major-Domo's mace, and the doors were flung wide, and the Major-Domo bellowed:

'Ladies and gentlemen! His Royal Highness the Prince of Wales!'

Seven

The Left-luggage Ticket

The Prince of Wales was a stout middle-aged gentleman wearing evening dress, with a grey beard and a cigar. He was accompanied by half a dozen grand-looking lords and ladies and swells all covered in medals and ribbons and ostrich feathers and monocles and diamond studs. And on either side of the Prince, looking triumphant, came Angela and Zerlina.

The appearance of the royal party caused a sensation. Ladies curtseyed, gentlemen bowed, and the Light Bombardiers played 'God Save the Queen'.

Benny nudged Thunderbolt.

'See?' he whispered. 'Never bet against the twins. They're blooming supernatural, they are.'

'But what are we going to do about—'

'Shh! Wait.'

And Benny put his finger to his lips, because the Prince of Wales had put down his cigar and was looking around genially.

'Thank you for your kind reception,' said the Prince to everyone in general. 'These two young ladies came to see my Private Secretary this morning and told us all about the ball, and we couldn't resist. But what's going on here? Are you playing charades?'

Everyone was too shy to answer. With an effort Inspector Gorman of the Yard swallowed his amazement and said, 'Er – no, Your Royal Highness, sir. We just apprehended this villain in the act of committing assault and battery, sir. He escaped from prison last night, sir.'

'Bless my soul,' said the Prince of Wales. 'And I hear you had a burglary here? Frightful bad luck. Lose a lot?'

The Worshipful Master of the Gas-Fitters' Company stepped forward and bowed.

'All our silver, Your Royal Highness. Over ten thousand pounds' worth of irreplaceable antiques.'

'Good Lord,' said the Prince. 'Caught the burglars yet, Inspector?'

'Well, Your Royal Highness——'

And at this point Mr Horspath seemed to ooze his way forward. Without actually stepping there, he appeared beside the inspector and bowed very deeply to the Prince of Wales.

'Albert Horspath,' he said in reverential tones. 'Deputy Gasworks Manager. If I may make an announcement, Your Royal Highness, we might get to the bottom of the mystery sooner than we had hoped.'

There was a ripple of excitement around the ballroom. Everyone was listening now; the waiters and the cooks and the musicians as well as all the guests were gaping open-mouthed at what was going on. It was as good as a play.

'Jolly good,' said the Prince. 'Carry on.'

'Thank you, sir,' said Mr Horspath, making a squirmy sort of bow. 'The fact is, I had not till this minute made the connection in my mind between what I saw the other night and the burglary itself. It was only seeing this rogue Smith here dressed in this suspicious way that reminded me.'

'You're a wavy-haired weasel!' shouted Dick.

'You keep quiet,' said the inspector. 'Carry on, Mr Horspath.'

'The other night,' said Mr Horspath, 'the night of the burglary, that is to say, I was taking my evening stroll when I saw this man climbing the fire-escape at the side of the building here.'

'You never did!' shouted Dick. 'You oily-eyed poodle-faker!'

'You hold your noise,' thundered the inspector. 'None of that forceful language! Don't you know who you're a-speaking in front of?'

Dick shut his mouth mutinously, and Mr Horspath, looking pious and sorrowful, went on:

'Yes, I saw him climbing the fire-escape with a sack on his back. Knowing that Mr Whittle keeps a pigeon-loft up there, I naturally assumed that he had employed Smith to look after his pigeons, and that Smith was carrying bird-seed or something of the sort. All we have to do is look, Inspector.'

Thunderbolt gasped at the wickedness of the man, but Benny whispered, 'Ssh! Wait! We ain't got him yet. Not quite.'

The Prince of Wales turned to the inspector.

'Sounds a simple enough suggestion, Inspector. Why don't you send a constable up to have a look round?'

'Off you go, Hopkins!' said the inspector, and a brisk-looking constable saluted smartly and ran off towards the stairs.

While they waited for him to come back, the guests whispered in excitement. Thunderbolt saw Mr Whittle looking very disturbed, and Miss Honoria holding his arm tightly.

Then they heard the constable's footsteps coming back at the double. He ran in, panting, saluted again, and said, 'Nothing there, sir. Just pigeons.'

There was a sigh of disappointment from everyone, but Benny was watching Mr Horspath. He saw him gulp and flick his eyes around swiftly before recovering himself.

'Obviously the rogue managed to move his ill-gotten booty away,' Mr Horspath said. 'You only have to interrogate him, Inspector.'

'I never done no such thing, you soapy serpent!' shouted Dick.

Benny took a deep breath and muttered to Thunderbolt, 'Here goes.'

Then he stepped forward.

Everyone's eyes turned to him, including the heavy-lidded ones belonging to the Prince of Wales. Benny felt the thrill of stardom.

'I know where it is,' he said.

There was a gasp from everyone, and the biggest one of all came from Mr Horspath.

'Oh, good evening, Your Royal Highness, sir,' Benny went on politely, because out of the corner of his eye he saw his father and mother gazing at him horrified, and thought he'd better be on his best behaviour.

'And who are you?' said the Prince.

'Benny Kaminsky, Your Royal Highness. I'm a detective,' Benny explained. 'And yesterday I was

doing some detecting and I happened to detect Mr Whittle going up to his pigeon-loft. I was in disguise so he probly don't know it was me.'

Everyone looked at Mr Whittle, and then back to Benny.

'Anyway, when I was there I detected that the Gas-Fitters' Hall silver *was* there, just like Mr Horspath said. I saw it behind the sacks of bird-seed.'

Mr Whittle's eyes had narrowed. As for Mr Horspath, he had gone very pale. But he nodded and said, 'I thought so. The boy's right. Oh, yes.'

And the policeman said, 'It

weren't there a minute ago, sir. I looked everywhere.'

'No,' said Benny, ''cause me and Thunderbolt moved it.'

Everyone gasped. Thunderbolt stepped forward and bowed very low to the Prince of Wales.

'This is Thunderbolt Dobney, Your Royal Highness,' said Benny. 'Me and him went up there last night and moved all the silver away to a place of safety, 'cause we reckoned that someone was trying to put the blame on someone else. We reckoned they was trying to put the blame on Mr Whittle, and we knew that Mr Whittle wouldn't nick the silver, 'cause that's ridiculous.'

'Thank you very much, Benny,' said Mr Whittle.

'So where is it?' said Inspector Gorman. 'What'd you do with it?'

Benny fished in his pocket and pulled out a crumpled scrap of paper.

'It's in the left-luggage office at Waterloo Station,' he said. 'Here's the ticket.'

'Cor!' said the twins at the same moment, in deep admiration.

The inspector took the ticket and gave it to the sergeant.

'Take a couple of men and nip round there quick,' he said. 'It's only five minutes away.'

The sergeant and two constables hurried away. The inspector turned back to Benny, looking fierce.

'Do you know that you have committed a grave offence?' he thundered. 'You oughter come and told the police immediately, instead of concealing the evidence! You could be severely punished for this!'

'Yeah, but if we done that,' said Thunderbolt, 'well, if we done that you'd never have found out who done the burglary.'

'And how are we going to find that out anyway?'

'It's obvious,' said Benny. 'The only person what knew the silver was there was the one as put it there in the first place. Mr Horspath, of course!'

Mr Horspath gave a ghastly grin, and then a merry laugh.

'Ha, ha!' he said. 'Jolly good yarn, Benny! Amusing, isn't it, sir?' he said to the Prince of Wales. 'I knew it was there because I saw that rotter Smith taking it up there, as I told you before, Inspector,' he added.

'We thought you'd say that,' said Benny. 'So we got someone else to come along. Your Royal Highness, may I present the famous escaped prisoner Sid the Swede?'

The Arab Chieftain stepped forward, lifting the robe to avoid falling over again. He took off the head-dress, and there was Sid the Swede.

'Benny told me as I'd probly get off if I told the truth,' he said shakily. 'I hope he's right, Your Majesty.'

The Prince of Wales raised his eyebrows.

'We'll see about that,' said Inspector Gorman. 'Well, Sid? What's your part in this affair?'

'Well, sir,' said Sid, twisting his fingers together, 'about a fortnight ago, sir, that gentleman come to me with a hoffer.'

He pointed to Mr Horspath.

'With a what?' said the Prince.

'With a hoffer of

hemployment, sir. He had a little job for me. He give me a few shillings and he hasked me to purchase a sack for him, sir.'

'Ha, ha, ha!' laughed Mr Horspath. 'Jolly good joke! Ha ha!'

'Why didn't he buy it hisself?' said the inspector.

'I think he didn't want it generally known as he was in the market for sacks, Your Honour. Anyway, I took the money, and then I fell into temptation, sir.'

'Temptation?' said the Prince.

'I'm afraid so, sir. Snake-Eyes – I mean, Mr Melmott was hoffering some very generous hodds in a sporting matter, and I laid it all on young D— I mean on the orse of my choice, sir. So once I'd done that, I had no money left and no sack neither, sir. So you see the dilemma what I was in, Your Royal Ighness.'

'Very tricky indeed,' said the Prince. 'So what did you do?'

'I done what any man would have done in the circumstances, Your Royal Ighness. I raided a washing line.'

'Yes, yer did, didn't yer!' came a voice from the crowd, and the people nearby turned to look at the stout and purple form of Mrs Liza Pearson. When she realized that everyone was looking at her, including the Prince of Wales, she became even purpler, and curtseyed. 'Begging your pardon, Your Royal Highness, but I saw this sneaking snivelling scoundrel making off with my washing. I couldn't give chase at the time, being up to me elbows in suds, but I caught im later round the Dog and Duck and gave im in charge. They oughter sent im down for ten year at least!'

'What did he steal?' said the Prince.

'He stole a pillow-case, Your Royal Highness!' she said, quivering with indignation.

'Yes, I did, sir, I admit it,' said Sid the Swede, nodding rapidly. 'And I give it to *im* instead of the sack as he wanted me to get.'

He pointed to Mr Horspath, who laughed heartily.

'Oh, this is rich!' Mr Horspath said. 'What a yarn, sir! Ha ha ha!'

'Yes, indeed,' said the Prince of Wales. 'I'm enjoying it immensely. And I think I can hear your men coming back, Inspector. I wonder what they've found.'

And everyone turned to the ballroom doors. No great star of the theatre or the music hall had ever had a more dramatic entrance than the sergeant and the two constables. They came puffing in carrying a great big canvas sack marked JOBSON'S HORSE NUTS and put it down with a clank.

'But you see,' cried Mr Horspath, 'that's a sack! An ordinary sack!'

'Well, course it is,' said Benny. 'We couldn't leave it in the left-luggage office in just a pillow-case, could we?'

'Open it up, Sergeant,' said the inspector.

The sergeant stopped mopping his brow and untied the length of hairy string around the neck of the sack. Benny knew what was in it, of course, so he couldn't resist looking at the effect it was all having on the guests. He'd never seen such wide eyes in his life – hundreds of them, all peering at the sack. It was marvellous.

'Here it is, Inspector!' said the sergeant, and pulled out a dirty white bag, and from the bag took out a gleaming silver gas-worker's wrench on an ebony plinth.

'The silver!' cried the Worshipful Master. 'The Jabez Calcutt Memorial Trophy!'

'My pillow-case!' cried Mrs Liza Pearson.

More and more silver was coming out of the pillow-case: great big dishes, cups, goblets, trays, salt-cellars. It gleamed and shone and glittered, and the only person who wasn't delighted was Mr Horspath.

He was looking ghastly pale. A fearful sweat stood out on his forehead, and his wavy hair hung in limp strands over his ears. But he still had enough presence of mind to laugh.

'Ha, ha! Jolly good jape! I hope you're going to put that young rascal away for a long time, Inspector. Slandering my reputation is a serious matter. I shall be consulting my lawyers in the morning.'

The Prince of Wales was never happy for long without a cigar in his hand, and having put his last one down more than twenty minutes ago, he was impatient for another. As he lifted it to his lips Mr Horspath darted to his side, matchbox in hand, and struck a light for him.

'Here you are, sir! Allow me!' he said.

And as soon as he'd lit the cigar, Benny darted to him and snatched the matchbox away.

'What are you doing?' said Mr Horspath. 'Look at him, Inspector! A common little sneak-thief! He can't leave anything alone!'

But Benny wasn't listening. He was intent on fishing a screw of paper out of his pocket, and taking out a match, and comparing the length of it with Mr Horspath's.

'That's it!' he cried in triumph. 'We got him! This is the final proof!'

And he danced around like a mad thing.

The Prince of Wales puffed at his cigar and said, 'When you've finished dancing, would you mind explaining, young man?'

'We found this dead lucifer under the window in the alley where he got in! And it's a Swedish one, and they're longer'n English matches! And *he's* been to Sweden, and the one he's just lit the cigar with is the same! It's him, and we proved it!'

And that was too much for Mr Horspath. Seeing

himself finally trapped, he gave a wild cry and rushed for the thinnest part of the crowd, meaning to escape.

But unluckily for him, the thinnest part of the crowd was where Henry the Eighth was standing, and as Mr Horspath tried to dodge past, the famous king reached out a mighty hand and grabbed him. Mr Horspath wriggled like a maggot, he squealed like a pig, but he was caught.

'Where d'you think you're going?' said Henry the Eighth, and the twins cried, 'Orlando!'

'Yus, it's me,' said Orlando. 'Here you are, Inspector, take your prisoner.'

The policemen put some handcuffs on Mr Horspath, who snarled villainously.

'Well, this seems to have ended very happily,' said the Prince of Wales. 'May I congratulate the young detectives?'

He shook hands with Benny and Thunderbolt.

'Er—' said Sid the Swede. 'I was just wondering, you know—'

'Yeah, what about Sid?' said Benny. 'He come here at the risk of more imprisonment so's he could help catch Mr Horspath, didn't he? So you oughter let him go!'

'Ah, but he broke out of prison,' said the inspector. 'So did young Dick here. That's a serious matter on its own.'

And Orlando stepped forward in his Henry the Eighth costume and bowed to the Prince.

'I have a confession to make,' he said. 'It was me what helped 'em break out. My name is Orlando, Your Royal Highness, perfessional strong man. I climbed up a ladder and I got hold the bars like *that* – and I wrenched 'em like *that* – and I heaved and I twisted like *that* – till there was room for 'em to get out. So part of the blame is mine, Your Royal Highness. And if there's handcuffs what can hold me, I shall be honoured to put my hands in 'em.'

Angela looked at Zerlina, and Zerlina looked at Angela.

'Well,' said Angela, 'really . . .'

'It was our idea all the time,' said Zerlina.

'And we nicked the ladder out of Charlie Ladysmith's yard . . .'

'And we woke Orlando up by throwing stones at him.'

'Oh, I'm used to that,' said Orlando, in case anyone thought the twins had been cruel. 'You seen the act, Your Royal Highness? The best bit is where they bounce cannon-balls off me head. I'll send you a ticket. I reckon I oughter pay me debt to society now. But,' he said dramatically, 'before I go inside, I got an announcement to make.'

He took off the Henry the Eighth hat and beard and looked properly like Orlando again, and then he said:

'Some time ago I fell in love with a young lady. I done everything I could to please her, like crushing rocks and eating yards of anchor-chain, but I never had the nerve to do what I really wanted to do and propose to her. And seeing as she's here tonight, I'd like to do it here and now afore I lose me nerve.'

And he got to one knee and held out his hands to Miss Honoria Whittle.

'Honoria, will you be my wife?' he said. 'Will you share the rough-and-ready life of a perfessional strong man?'

'Oh, Orlando! Of course I will!'

And the band, who'd been following everything, played a loud chord of C Major as the two of them embraced.

Thunderbolt was amazed.

'So *he's* the one with the love phoby!' he said. 'Miss Whittle said she knew someone else with one – just like Dick!'

And that reminded everyone of Dick, who stood there still under police guard, together with Sid the Swede, who'd been re-arrested.

Then Benny had an inspiration.

'Excuse me, Your Royal Highness,' he said. 'Seeing as we've detected the real burgular, and seeing as we couldn't of done it without Sid the Swede, and seeing as Dick was only inside for clocking Mr Horspath one on the razzo when he made up to Daisy behind the potted palm, what about a Royal Pardon?'

The Prince of Wales considered it, puffing at his cigar and eyeing Benny thoughtfully.

'Properly speaking, you ought to apply to Her Majesty the Queen,' he said. 'But in the circumstances I am sure she would agree to your request. Release them, Inspector!'

And the police unlocked the handcuffs. Sid the Swede slunk away to avoid Mrs Pearson, and Dick stood blinking with embarrassment in the centre of a cheering circle of friends and neighbours, clapping him on the back and shaking his hand.

Then someone said, 'Go on, Dick! Ask her!'

And someone else yelled, 'Here she is! Go it, Dick!'

And there was Daisy, looking bashful. Everyone was

looking on and grinning, including the policemen, because some of them had had a quiet bet with Snake-Eyes Melmott, too. The only one who didn't know what it was all about was the Prince of Wales, but Angela plucked his sleeve and whispered to him, and he smiled.

And Dick stood there getting redder and redder. He looked down at the floor; he looked up at the ceiling. He opened his mouth – he closed it again.

He looked around for escape, just as Mr Horspath had done.

'Oh no,' whispered Thunderbolt. 'He's not gonna do it . . .'

Then the Prince of Wales bent and whispered something to Zerlina, who scampered around and plucked at the sleeve of the band-leader and whispered something to *him*; and the band-leader said something to the band, and they raised their instruments, took a deep breath, and began to play.

And everyone recognized the tune, and laughed and joined in:

'Daisy, Daisy, give me your answer, do!
I'm half crazy, all for the love of you;
It won't be a stylish marriage –
I can't afford a carriage;
But you'll look sweet, upon the seat
Of a bicycle made for two!'

And the loudest singing of all came from Dick, and by the time the song was over, somehow he had proposed, and somehow she had accepted, and they stood there blushing like two tomatoes and looking very happy.

'Well, my congratulations to the happy couples,' said the Prince of Wales.

And he shook hands with Dick, and with Daisy and Miss Whittle, who both curtseyed. And then he held out his hand to Orlando.

'Ah,' said Orlando. 'Now I'd like to shake your hand, sir, but I daren't. You see, this hand of mine can crush rocks.'

'You crush rocks with your hand?' said the Prince. 'I bet you can't.'

'Did I hear you say *bet*, Your Royal Highness?' said

a rich and fruity voice. 'May I offer my services?'

'Snake-Eyes Melmott!' said Angela.

The famous bookmaker had appeared as if by magic, with his little black book in hand.

'I can offer odds in the matter of rock-crushing to any lady or gentleman present,' he said, and within a minute he was doing a brisk trade. The Prince of Wales bet ten guineas that Orlando couldn't, and Mr Whittle bet ten guineas that he could, and dozens of other bets were entered in the little black book. Angela and Zerlina were watching closely. It turned out that more people thought that Orlando couldn't than thought he could, so if he could, Snake-Eyes Melmott would win. And since he hardly ever lost, that would have been the way to bet – if the gang had had any money to bet with.

'I wish he'd paid out on the other bet first,' said Thunderbolt. 'Then I could've put all me winnings on Orlando and won a *fortune*.'

When all the bets were laid, a space was cleared in the centre of the dance-floor, and a servant came in with a silver tray covered in a snowy white napkin, in the middle of which was a rock the size of an orange.

'Right,' said Orlando. 'Now you better all stand back a bit, on account of flying chips of rock.'

Miss Whittle kissed him for luck, and he rolled up his sleeves to reveal the biggest muscles anyone had ever seen. He took the rock in his right hand, weighing it carefully. From the band came a low roll on the snare drum.

Orlando raised the rock high. The drumbeat got louder.

He gritted his teeth. The veins stood out on his head. He began to squeeze. The muscles in his arm bulged even bigger. The drumbeat got louder still.

And then the rock began to crumble. A trail of powder fell to the floor, and suddenly there was nothing in Orlando's hand but bits of gravel and sand. There was a crash from the cymbals, an even louder chord of C Major from the band, and everyone cheered and clapped, including the Prince of Wales.

Orlando brushed his hands together and bowed. The gang watched Snake-Eyes Melmott paying out to those who'd won.

'H'mm,' said Benny. 'Well, at least we'll get our winnings from the main bet.'

And while most of the guests were dancing or eating or drinking toasts to the newly engaged couples, a line of eager punters was forming at one side of the ballroom to get their money from Snake-Eyes Melmott. Everyone who'd put money on Dick was there, from Sid the Swede to the local vicar.

Thunderbolt could hardly contain his excitement. All that money! And beating Snake-Eyes Melmott!

But it seemed as if there was a problem. Thunderbolt stopped grinning and listened.

'Ladies and gentlemen,' Snake-Eyes was saying, 'may I introduce the well-known and highly respected timekeeper, Mr Bell, known to members of the boxing fraternity as Ding-Dong. Ding-Dong Bell's timekeeping is known to be immaculate, which is why I invited him along this evening to make a careful note of the proceedings in case there was any dispute about the finish. Mr Bell.'

Ding-Dong Bell was a thin, scholarly-looking man with no less than three different kinds of watch. He placed them all on the table in front of him.

'Them watches,' he said, 'was synchronized by me personal, to the chimes of Big Ben, at six o'clock last. And according to them, young Dick's proposal, as noted by two independent witnesses, took place at five minutes past midnight.'

'Well, ladies and gentlemen,' said Snake-Eyes Melmott, 'what a shame, what a shame! You all remember the terms of the bet:

Dick had to propose and be accepted before twelve o'clock. So I'm afraid you all lost. However, the good news is I'm opening a book on the likelihood of living dinosaurs being discovered in the South American jungle by the Royal Geographical Expedition. I can offer you a hundred to one against a pterodactyl – how's that? Can't say fairer than that. Hundred to one, gents! Any takers?'

With cries of disappointment and dismay the people turned away, tearing up their betting slips and shaking their heads at their own folly.

'We should of known,' said Angela darkly.

'I could of sworn we had him this time!' said Zerlina.

'We'll get him yet. He's not beating us like that . . .'

Thunderbolt and Benny looked at each other. Their disgust was almost too deep for words.

'Cor,' said Benny finally. 'I mean to say, well, *blimey*.'

Thunderbolt couldn't say anything. The future was clear to him: gambling, drink, loose women, ruin, prison, the gallows. If only he'd paid more attention to 'The Primrose Path, or If Only He Had Known'!

He gulped. It was going to be very hard to tell

Miss Whittle that he couldn't pay her; never mind telling Pa . . .

There was a slight cough, and they looked around. Mr Whittle stood there, with the Worshipful Master of the Ancient and Worshipful Company of Gas-Fitters.

'Young gents,' said the Worshipful Master, 'and young ladies too, I understand. Commendable ingenuity and initiative. Daring and resourceful plan. On behalf of the Ancient and Worshipful Company of Gas-Fitters, I should be proud to offer you a reward of ten pounds each, and invite you all to partake of ice-cream with His Royal Highness the Prince of Wales. If you would care to step this way . . .'

And everything was all right, just like that.

So the New Cut Gang sat down with the Prince of Wales, and watched Orlando dancing with Miss Whittle, and Dick dancing with Daisy, and the silver gleaming on the sideboard, and Mr Miller showing three young men how to keep themselves cool by the application of cucumber, and everyone having a whale of a time.

'I think this is probably the social event of the

Season,' said the Prince of Wales. 'Thank you for inviting me to the Gas-Fitters' Ball.'

'It was a pleasure,' said Angela. 'By the way . . .'

'I don't suppose you know where we can get a pterodactyl?' said Zerlina.

Philip Pullman is one of the most highly respected children's authors writing today. Winner of many prestigious awards, including the Carnegie of Carnegies and the Whitbread Award, Pullman's epic fantasy trilogy *His Dark Materials* has been acclaimed as a modern classic. It has sold 17.5 million copies worldwide and been translated into 40 languages. In 2005 he was awarded the Astrid Lindgren Memorial Award. He lives in Oxford.